THE SHEIKH'S
SECRET BABY

DIANA FRASER

The Sheikh's Secret Baby
by Diana Fraser

© 2020 Diana Fraser

A controlling sheikh with a secret, a beautiful model with a broken heart, forced into a marriage to save their son. But can it save their love?

—The Sheikhs of Havilah—
The Sheikh's Secret Baby
Bought by the Sheikh
The Sheikh's Forbidden Lover

—Desert Kings—
Wanted: A Wife for the Sheikh
The Sheikh's Bargain Bride
The Sheikh's Lost Lover
Awakened by the Sheikh
Claimed by the Sheikh
Wanted: A Baby by the Sheikh

For more information about this author, visit:
http://www.dianafraser.net

PROLOGUE

$\mathcal{B}$eneath the lazy whirls of the overhead fan, the three kings sat around the pitted and well-polished medieval table, a beloved remnant of when the three kingdoms had been one country—the fabled land of Havilah.

The table—like the cavernous hall of the desert hunting lodge in which the three men met monthly to discuss the issues upon which the future prosperity of their kingdoms depended—represented their joint history, and their joint future.

"The king of Jazira continues to turn a blind eye to the incursions his people make upon ours," said Sheikh Amir al-Rahman, his eyes narrowing with controlled anger.

"The hatred runs too deep and for too many centuries to ever disappear," said Sheikh Zavian bin Ameen Al Rasheed. "We have what they want—wealth."

Sheikh Roshan al-Haidar leaned back in his chair, looking every inch the playboy beloved of western media. "Our only hope continues to be with the king of Tawazun. A strong union with his country would bring balance to the region. Jazira wouldn't dare antagonize us with Tawazun's might behind us.

"You're right, Roshan. And Tawazun's traditional culture means marriage is the only truly binding way to achieve this."

A silence fell upon the great hall as each king considered what this meant for them. It was Roshan who broke the silence, leaning forward, his arms upon the table, eyeing Amir and Zavian in turn.

"We made a blood oath to build an enduring peace for Havilah no matter what the price. And that means one of us must marry one of the Tawazun sheikha. Preferably the eldest." Roshan's gaze settled on Amir. "You volunteered. Have you made any progress?"

A muscle twitched in Amir's jaw, the only sign of the agitation he felt within. Both men noticed it.

"No. I have... other matters to consider over the next few months. I told you about my son's health. I need to deal with this before I can pursue marriage."

The others nodded. "Have you found a suitable donor for Hani?" asked Zavian.

"Yes. His mother," said Amir. There were no secrets between the three men.

Zavian grunted. "I see. That sounds... complicated. Well, we'll leave it with you, but keep us updated. This issue cannot continue for much longer. If you cannot do this, then the task must fall to me or Roshan." He paused. "None of us want another war."

The grim specter of war silently hung over them as the meeting concluded.

Outside the hunting lodge, under the fierce light and scorching heat of the central desert region which adjoined each of their three countries, three helicopters waited to return the kings to their countries.

As-Salaam Alaykum, murmured the kings, before they went their separate ways.

Peace be with you, repeated Amir to himself as the helicopter door slid closed behind him.

Somehow he didn't think the next few months would bring him peace, in any shape or form…

CHAPTER 1

Milan

"*A* letter? For me?" Ruby Armand shouted, trying to make herself heard above the thumping beat of the nightclub.

"*Si!*" The stranger thrust it into her hand and disappeared into the sea of people who rose and fell as one to the pulsing beat.

"You receiving your post in nightclubs now?" Raife's breath tickled her ear. She moved away.

"Apparently." She twisted the letter in her hand so the writing could catch the light. There was nothing except her name.

"A billet-doux, perhaps?" Raife smiled. "A love letter from a stranger or from someone you know?"

"No idea. There's no indication who it's from."

"Then open it."

Ruby tapped the envelope on the table. Her thumb smoothed over thick, embossed paper. She rarely received letters any more—just short electronic one-liners. Certainly not letters in expensive envelopes. "I…" She trailed off as she placed it in her bag, for some reason unwilling to open it in public. "I'll go to the rest room. The light is better there."

Raife flashed the smile that had made him the highest paid model in Italy and turned his attention to someone else. It didn't concern Ruby. She had many friends, many admirers, but few were close, and even fewer were indispensable.

Once in the elegant restroom she sat down and slid her finger along the barely sealed envelope. Suddenly a group of women burst in and clustered around the mirror, applying lipstick, running their fingers through long, sun-kissed hair and talking over each other. Their conversation stuttered as they gave her a second glance—everyone always did, she was instantly recognizable from the countless fashion shoots she'd done, countless gossip columns she'd featured in— before they turned back to the mirror and resumed talking.

Ruby walked into one of the toilets and closed the door. She hooked up her bag, leaned against the wall and pulled one solitary piece of paper from the envelope. It was a short note, just a couple of paragraphs, with an embossed coat of arms in one corner. She scanned down to the signature.

Amir Al-Rahman.

Her heart raced. Amir? After all these years?

She skimmed the letter and frowned, not understanding the words at first. She read through again, slowly this time. Her eyes stopped on the words "our son". Her mouth dried and the paper slipped from her hands as a sob—loud and naked—escaped her lips. The chatter outside the toilet stopped instantly. But she didn't make any further sound, just stared at the elaborate wallpaper as the memories she constantly tried to suppress surged into her mind.

"Are you okay?" one of the girls called out.

It was only when she relaxed her mouth from framing the noiseless sob that the tears began to roll down her face. "I'm fine, thanks," she answered, pressing the palm of her hand against her pounding forehead, as she tried to contain the shock that she'd found her son after all these years.

She tried to stop the gasping sobs that now threatened to overwhelm her, but bile rose and she turned and vomited into the toilet. Shakily she wiped her mouth, ran cold water into the sink and splashed her face. She gripped the sides of the basin and looked up at her reflection in the mirror.

Her long blonde hair still framed her face, her skin was still translucent, a favorite with photographers, but her eyes had changed. Swimming with tears and fear—fear that she'd found what she'd been searching for these past five years, only for it to be taken away. Because of all the scenarios that had haunted her, Amir Al-Rahman—her baby's father—having adopted their son, even *knowing* about their son, had never crossed her mind.

~

Ten minutes until she arrived.

SHEIKH AMIR AL-RAHMAN drummed his fingers on the side of the solid oak chair and tried to concentrate on what his assistant was saying. He *never* had to try to concentrate. Just the thought of seeing Ruby again was fracturing his control. He stopped drumming and gripped the chair.

"Leave me."

His executive assistant stopped talking mid-sentence and opened his eyes in surprise. "But the—"

Amir narrowed his eyes. It was all he had to do to make the man collect the papers and rise. *No one* questioned him. He'd inherited his kingdom, one-third of the fabled Havilah lands, from his father and *his* father before him, and had absolute control of it. "Leave now. And make sure I'm not disturbed after Miss Armand arrives." The flustered assistant nodded obsequiously and walked out the room. The deep silence of the private wing of the ancient palace settled around him once more.

Five minutes.

He didn't need to check the time. He'd been aware of each passing minute from the moment he'd awoken, as if his body clock was set on an alarm, programmed to go off on her arrival.

He opened his laptop—the only concession to modernity in the library—responded to a couple of emails and closed the computer once more.

One minute.

He tapped his fingertips lightly together as he focused on the pale blue spring sky and the distant sound of a car entering the inner compound of the palace. Suddenly it was real. What he'd imagined in weak moments over the past five years was about to happen.

He shifted the photos of his dark-haired wife and blond son on his desk, his gaze lingering on his son, Hani. He regretted it instantly. He felt the pain seep into him like a bruise receiving a further blow, sending the blood further into his body, wounding and hurting. The boy's pallor had always concerned him and now he knew why. But he would deal with it, like he dealt with everything else.

The car stopped outside the front entrance and two sets of footsteps approached: one barely heard, the other sharp-heeled against the ancient stone floor, growing louder as they came towards him, keeping time with the increased tempo of his pounding heart. Both sets of footsteps stopped, followed by a tentative knock at the door.

"Enter!"

The door opened and his assistant let her in. The smell of her perfume—the same as it had always been, despite the fact she could now afford the best—wafted over to him. He rose and turned to her slowly, intent on retaining the control that simply her presence threatened. And he needed all that control when he looked into her eyes, because they were the eyes of a stranger.

He'd seen photos, more than he'd wanted—of course he had. She was as glamorous as the magazines portrayed her. He knew how she wore her long blonde hair—often in an upswept messy bun which suited her delicate features—and knew her preference for bright, bold, sexy clothes. Today was no exception. She was dressed in a short, tight shift dress, the color of sunshine. But she was taller in her high heels, her figure slighter than it had been five years before, and her skin wasn't pale, but had a soft golden tan that made her bright blue eyes appear almost violet.

Superficially, all was as he'd expected. What he hadn't anticipated was the change in the expression of her eyes. Five years ago, they'd been full of fun, life and love. Now they held only hostility and anger. They were hard.

She dropped the fashionably large handbag with a clunk onto the floor, walked up to the desk, gripped it—the chunky gold bracelet falling to her wrist, hitting the hard surface of the desk with a clatter—and leaned over, her eyes fierce.

"Where's my son?"

Lust slammed into his gut at the feel of her so close, her lips, full and soft with the gloss of coral lipstick, and the long lines of her slender arms in the sleeveless dress that glanced off subtle curves. He hadn't expected that blast of need. It was as if his body had an elastic memory, like a form of plastic that, when subjected to a heat source, resumes its original form. It made him feel vulnerable. It made him feel angry. It banished the turmoil.

"Sit down." His voice held its usual strength and command. He was not used to being disobeyed and didn't expect it. He *would* get what he wanted.

"No. Not until you tell me where my son is."

"Sit down and I might consider it."

"Might?" She cocked her head to one side, her fine brows arched in an arrogant question. "Might? Don't tell me you've brought me all this way for some other reason." She brought her head closer to his, her eyes ranging over his face, faltering slightly. "Because"—she drew back, suddenly less sure—"I won't believe it."

"Sit down, Miss Armand."

She continued to pull away slowly, even as her eyes moved over his face. He could see she was checking him out, just as he was checking her out. The glint of hardness faded a little, and, as she turned to find a chair, she nipped her bottom lip. But, by the time she'd turned back, crossed her slim legs and folded her hands in front of her, the small sign of uncertainty had vanished.

"'*Miss Armand*'," she repeated. "Why so formal? Have you forgotten the name of the mother of your child?"

"I know the name of the mother of my child. Her name was Mia."

"*That's* the name of the woman you left me for. That's the name of your wife. That is *not* the name of my son's mother."

He held her hard stare. "Mia was, as I say, my child's mother. You forfeited that right when you signed the adoption papers. You'd made it clear you didn't want him."

For a moment, when he caught sight of her shocked expression before she turned away, he almost regretted the words. They'd meant to hurt. And they had. But he didn't usually deal such low blows.

"You don't understand. I made a mistake, I was sick, I—"

"No excuses. You signed your rights away, left the hospital and didn't look back."

Anger sparked into her eyes and she jumped up. "Don't you *dare* tell me I didn't look back. I've been trying for years to track him down. And I've been blocked. Every time I've gone to the records office, I've had some clerk look at me like I'm dirt and tell me absolutely nothing."

He rarely felt regret but he couldn't soften. That was what she did—wormed her way under your skin, into your soul and before you knew it, you were at her mercy. He shrugged. "But he wasn't adopted. I *am* his father. After I discovered his existence and my paternity was confirmed by a DNA test, I added my name to the birth certificate. There was no need for me and my wife to adopt him. You made your decision and all I was doing was making sure you abided by it."

She exhaled roughly and looked around, as if for some reason, some escape, some explanation. She turned and paced away, pushed her fingers through her hair, seemed to regain her control and strode back to him. "I just wanted to know he was okay, that he was cared for."

"I had no interest in what you wanted." He watched his cold words take effect. They sparked her into an anger that didn't threaten to break his resolve. Anger he could deal with, coldness he could deal with.

"No. It was always about what *you* wanted, wasn't it? You wanted sex with me, then you wanted to marry Mia. You got both. And a child into the bargain. How neatly it all worked out for you."

He ground his teeth. "Neatly?" He clenched and unclenched his fist. He couldn't lose his temper.

"Yes, neatly. Everything you do, you do for a purpose.

11

Your life is one huge chess game. You plan everything; you control everything."

"Of course. Without control there's only chaos. And you'd know all about that, wouldn't you?"

"Don't go criticizing—"

He held up his hand. "Sit down, Ruby. Be quiet. We have things to discuss."

"You don't say?"

He watched her anger fade as she realized he was right. Slowly she withdrew her hands from the desk and sat down. But he could still see the tension in her lightly wrung hands and in her eyes that hadn't moved from his.

"Just tell me this," she continued. "Why the hell didn't you inform me you'd taken him? Why?" she repeated.

"You're not here to ask questions. You're here at my invitation, because I want you to be."

"I want to see him." Her chin jutted forward in a mulish air of determination. A battle of will over emotion played out over her trembling lips.

He opened his mouth to speak but hesitated. It suddenly occurred to him that she might be more upset than he'd imagined she'd be. It was a small thought that winkled its way to some soft place he didn't know he had. He cleared his throat. "And you can. But first there are things to discuss."

She nodded. "Okay. But first, tell me. Was Mia good to him?"

"She loved him. Treated him as if he were her own."

"Good." She looked away, and then back at him. "I was sorry, you know. Sorry to hear about Mia."

"Were you?"

"Of course. You think me so heartless I wouldn't be sorry she'd died in a car accident?"

"I think you so heartless that you'd willingly rid yourself of our child, without even telling me about Hani."

He watched her pale beneath her tan. "Hani…" she said softly. "Hani." Her outstretched hand trembled. "So you use the name I gave him. Is it because you knew it was special, that it was my father's name?"

He did, of course, but he'd rather lie than allow her to realize this trace of sentiment. "My wife liked the name."

She nodded slowly and swiped her hand across her brow. The energy had suddenly left her and she inhaled a long, deep breath. "So, what's this all about? Why now? Mia's been dead a year. It can't be connected with her. What is it you want? Because I'm sure it's not for *my* satisfaction I've been invited here."

"So astute." It had seemed easy to bring her here before he'd seen her again. Seeing her made everything so much harder. "It's because I need to buy something from you."

"What can I possibly have that you want?"

"Something… very personal."

She shook her head, frowning. "What are you talking about?"

"My son—"

"*Our* son."

"He needs something from you."

"What?"

"All in good time."

"For pity's sake, Amir, let me see him."

He nodded to the window. "You can see him from there, for now."

She looked at him briefly, with a complex expression of intense longing and fear, before walking swiftly to the window, her hands gripping the deep window ledge as she leaned forward scanning the garden. Suddenly she was very still. Then she pushed the large casement window open to the courtyard outside, and the sound of Hani's laughter

13

drifted into the room. Her body tensed and he heard a sound like a sob as she slumped against the window frame.

Before he knew it he was standing behind her. But he couldn't bridge the distance of five years so easily. He simply watched as her hand rose, following Hani's progress as he chased a ball and disappeared beyond a high hedge.

She swayed slightly—as if that small glimpse was too much, coming after so little—and turned away from the window, not aware he was so close. She reached out to steady herself and pressed the flat of her hand against his chest. It shook him to the core.

"Ruby…"

She closed her eyes, and he gripped her hand and pressed it tighter against his chest. Her warm breath teased his cheek, sending a ripple of awareness through his body. It was like flicking a switch that had lain dormant for five long years. But before he could bring her closer, before he could obey the commands of his body, she pulled away, stepped to one side, pulling her hand away from his, confusion in her eyes and in her movements.

He felt the withdrawal like the cold, sharp, devastating withdrawal of an addiction. Five minutes in the room and he was putty in her hands.

She shook her head. "I'm okay. I don't need your support. All I need is Hani."

He allowed himself to inhale her light floral fragrance— bright and delicious, just like her—before he stepped away. He walked back to his desk, fighting for control. "Would you care for coffee?"

She sighed. "Sure. If that's what it'll take for me to see him."

He ordered the coffees and watched as she walked back to her seat and sat down, a different woman now the anger had left her.

She looked up at him with eyes that were no longer hard, but revealed a depth of emotion which made his heart thump heavily. "Tell me about him. Tell me about Hani. What's he like?"

He swallowed and forced himself to focus. "He's a good boy. Although he prefers playing to studying."

For the first time she looked at him with something like the old expression in her eyes, bright, full of fun. Her lips curled into a sweet smile. "I guess you wouldn't understand that. I can picture you as a boy Hani's age—studious, responsible, dutiful. Some things don't change, do they?"

"I hope Hani's attitude to his studies changes."

"It will, when he finds what interests him." She paused as if trying to frame an important question. "Can I see him? Not just through the window, I mean, but meet him?"

"Not yet."

Anger flamed once more in her eyes. "Dammit, Amir! Stop punishing me. Is it so hard to understand why I agreed to an adoption? Hey? You'd told me in no uncertain terms we had no future, and that you were to marry another woman. I hardly thought you'd welcome the news that you'd made me pregnant. I hardly thought I owed you anything at all."

"Not even the truth?"

"Least of all the truth. I still don't understand how you knew about him—who told you? So few people knew."

He sighed. "Ah, Ruby, you underestimate the power attached to wealth and royalty."

"You weren't Italian royalty."

"I didn't need to be. My grandfather established business links with Milan which I still retain. People knew of our relationship, and I was told about Hani. Did you really believe I wouldn't find out?" But he could see from her eyes that she had. He shook his head in disbelief. "You'd discharged yourself by the time the DNA test confirmed I was his father. I had a new birth certificate issued and he came home with Mia and me. Anyway, I haven't brought you here to talk about the past."

"Then tell me why I'm here."

"He's ill."

"Hani's ill? He looked fine. What's the matter with him?"

"His kidneys aren't functioning well. He needs a blood transfusion. I'm not a match but you should be."

She gasped. "A blood transfusion?" She shook her head in confusion. "But why me? Why bring me here when it's obvious you'd have preferred not to? You could find suitable blood anywhere."

He didn't speak immediately and her frown deepened. She wanted answers. She wouldn't be getting them. Not yet. "I don't wish to have a stranger's blood in my son." But he could see she wasn't satisfied with his answer. "It's… complicated."

She gasped and looked away, bringing her hand up to shield her eyes from his gaze. "How sick is he?" Her voice was a shadow of what it had been only moments before. He hadn't considered that she'd be upset.

"He's only recently been diagnosed with the beginnings of rare kind of kidney failure. A genetically profiled blood transfusion, together with a new drug is the recommended treatment. Further transfusions may be required."

She dropped her hand but her eyes were closed tight. "No."

"I expected that from someone who signed their son away." He sighed heavily with disappointment. "You *will* be paid."

She shook her head, hardly hearing what he was saying. "No," she repeated. "My son can't be sick."

"You really won't even do this for him, will you?"

She stared at him, incredulous. "I'll do anything to save him."

He exhaled roughly with derision. "You're not spinning tales to magazines now. I know you, Ruby. I *know* you. You're only interested in saving yourself."

She just shook her head. "You don't know me at all. You know nothing about me. I've been looking for him. I can't find him only to lose him again."

"I don't believe you." He scanned her face, trying to read her, but failed. "I don't trust your maternal instincts. You rejected him five years ago. Why would you help him now? You did nothing at his birth and you'll do nothing now." He opened a drawer, pulled out a check and slid it across to her. "You'll do nothing, unless you have an incentive."

RUBY LOOKED DOWN at the check. "One million dollars." She read the words out loud but they meant nothing. Her mind and heart were swirling with a confusion of feelings that just seeing Hani, just being with Amir again, had created in her. She hadn't even known the feelings were still there, but they'd surfaced as soon as she'd set eyes on him. And now this. To see Hani, and then to lose him? Impossible! She raised her eyes to Amir's. They were as hard as the black strokes that formed the words on the check.

"You really think you have to buy me?"

"You've shown me nothing to make me think otherwise. Take it. Providing tests on your blood are satisfactory, after the transfusion you can continue to do as you've been doing —live the high life, feature in all the magazines, leave a trail of lovers."

His expression had scarcely altered since she'd walked into the room. Whatever *she'd* said, whatever *he'd* said, his face had remained cold and impassive. He looked exactly the same as five years before—tall, powerful, with eyes so dark that one could lose oneself in them—but he'd never had this blank unfeeling control that chilled her to her bones. His voice was full of hate, full of bitterness. That he could truly believe she was so heartless, so cold and lacking in love, killed her.

"You hate me." The words slipped out. "Of course you do."

"I don't hate you." His voice remained low. He looked away with an uncharacteristic sideways glance. Then he appeared to collect himself. "Hate is too strong an emotion. It's the opposite of love." His eyes became cold once more. "I don't hate you. I'm indifferent."

"Indifference sounds deadlier."

He shrugged. "I feel sorry for you. Your life is one long circus of people, events, partying. One long search for excitement and entertainment."

"You've no idea what my life's been like. Don't begin to try to make up something about which you know nothing."

"I know. I've watched."

A chill shiver swept through her body before settling in her gut. He'd watched her every move these past five years and she hadn't known it. All this time she'd thought he'd forgotten about her existence, he'd been aware of her. She didn't query his claim. Despite what he thought, she was well aware of his power, which opened doors for him everywhere. Not only in his homeland of Janub Havilah, but also in Italy, where'd they'd met. But here he owned everything—from the stone walls of the palace, the ochre tones of the ancient roof tiles, to every square foot of land from border to border of this small middle eastern country.

"You may have watched, but you haven't understood." Slowly she rose and walked to the window. She couldn't sit opposite him any longer, looking into those eyes that were so cold to her. There was no sign of Hani in the garden now.

"I'm not interested in understanding you, Ruby. I'm interested in you only in as far as you can help Hani."

She turned to him, coolly. "You really are a bastard. You'd use anybody to further your own wishes, wouldn't you?"

"I get what I want."

"Then all I can say is I'm very happy you don't want me."

"Not then, and not now."

"I'm glad that's clear." She walked over to her bag and picked it up. "I take it you've no further revelations? If my blood is a match and nothing untoward is found in it, you want it—but you don't want my heart. Not that a million bucks would buy my heart."

"But it will undoubtedly buy your blood."

"Undoubtedly?" She shook her head, incredulous. What the hell had happened to him to believe that he could buy anybody or anything? His country and family had taken him and turned him into someone devoid of humanity, someone who thought everyone had a price.

"Of course. I've covered everything. I've left nothing to chance."

"You know? I'm tempted to exercise my mind, that you always found so chaotic, and find something you haven't covered—some eventuality that would throw you."

He shrugged. "Your prerogative. Amuse yourself how you wish."

She flashed him a brief smile. "I will. Now, where's Hani? I want to see him. Spend some time with him."

"Not until you agree to take the money."

She looked from him to the check and shook her head, still unable to believe he thought she could be bought. But, then, if taking the money was going to get her to see her son, so be it. Let him think what he wanted, she'd rip up the check as soon as she could. She reached out, took the check, folded

19

it in half and dropped it carelessly in her bag. "I agree. Now take me to him."

His lip curled and his eyes narrowed with contempt. Momentarily she felt his disdain cut into her. But, she reminded herself, it didn't matter. She'd lost his respect years ago. And there was nothing she could do about it.

He rose—the energy and sexuality of the man she once knew, contained now in that tall, powerful body—and opened the door. "This way."

She walked toward him and stopped—so close she could see his nostrils flare as he inhaled her. A wave of satisfaction flowed over her, and she smiled and leaned in to him. She brought her finger to the lapel of his jacket and ran it down its length. "One thing's changed about you. You dress better now."

"I've changed a lot more than that. I'm not the same man you once knew."

"Oh." She looked up at him suddenly and saw his brown eyes darken in response. "I think you are. You just hide it better."

Allowing a light smile to play on her lips, she walked out the door. He'd have seen—she knew he had. She was determined to play him at his own game. Yes, she was here for Hani. Yes, she'd do anything for him. And she was determined in the process to show Amir he was wrong. He thought he controlled everything. He'd made a mistake. He didn't control her and never would.

CHAPTER 2

The history of the Al-Rahman dynasty pressed around Ruby as if it were a physical thing. From the huge, ornate, gilded mirrors above onyx-topped tables to the floor-to-ceiling family portraits, there was no escaping their brooding presence. She glanced at Amir, who walked beside her in stony silence. It wasn't any sense of importance that gave him his aura of authority. It had nothing to do with his height and strength. He wore his power easily, as if he were unaware of it, as if it came naturally to him. He'd have been the same if he'd worked in a factory. She smiled. The thought was unimaginable.

Amir glanced at her. He held open a door to another room, full of heavy Victorian furniture and fittings. "You find the current situation amusing?"

"No." She passed through into the room. "Not at all. Just you."

She walked ahead of him but could feel his eyes on her back and suppressed a shiver, as if his gaze had touched her like a chill breeze. She stopped at the next door—there were no corridors that she could see, simply rooms opening up into other rooms—and he opened it for her. Their eyes met and she made sure a hint of a smile remained on her face, despite what she felt. But the smile faded under his disapproving stare. She was treading on dangerous ground.

"I realize it is hard for you behave in a rational manner, but I suggest you try. This is no laughing matter. Hani comes first." He didn't wait for her to pass through the door, but stepped into the sunshine and walked out onto the stone-flagged terrace which edged the private garden, looking inland away from the ocean. She followed him to its farthest edge, below which there was a wide expanse of pristine grass bordered by a high hedge.

"Believe me, Amir, I'm aware of the seriousness of the situation. Allow me to process this in my own way."

Amir glanced at her as if he were bored and then turned away. "Over there." Amir nodded. "Hani's playground is behind the hedge. He and his nanny are waiting for us."

They walked down the terrace steps and her heart began to race. So near after so many years searching. "Does he know I'm coming?"

"He knows a friend of mine is visiting and wishes to meet him."

"How on earth are we going to explain everything to him?"

He stopped suddenly and turned to her, his lip curled in disbelief. "You don't understand, do you? This isn't the beginning of something for you. You said goodbye to a relationship with my son years ago. There's nothing *to* explain to Hani. There will be *no* relationship. You can meet him now"—he shrugged—"perhaps a few more times before the hospital procedure. Then you will have your money and you will leave. Like you always do."

She looked away, biting back an angry retort. "Just let me see him now."

"Wait here."

He disappeared through a gap in the hedge and she followed him, stopping suddenly when she caught sight of the edge of a sandpit, complete with diggers, buckets and a waterspout that threatened to turn the sandpit into a mud bath. She could only see Amir, striding over to the sandpit. She waited in the shadows of the dark cypress hedge that blocked her vision of anyone but Amir. Her breath stopped. Her *son* was behind that hedge. Her *son*, after all these years.

"Hani!" She snapped her focus back to Amir. His voice had changed in an instant. It was softer and showed an emotion she wouldn't have believed possible based on the past half-hour. But it *was* there. Just not for her.

"Baba!"

Ruby clutched her mouth, as the sound of the small boy slammed into her. "It's only afternoon," the voice continued. "It's not our time yet! Come and see what I'm making."

She was shocked to hear Hani's high, musical voice—influenced by Amir's very proper Oxford-educated accent, and yet tinged with the exotic accent of Havilah. Somehow, in her imagination, Hani always had an Italian accent. But of course he wouldn't. He'd only been born, and no doubt holidayed, in Italy. He'd lived all his life here, between the Arabian Sea and the desert in Janub Havilah, the southern part of the ancient land of Havilah. She knew it, but the gap between her imagination and reality shocked her. Amir had all the influence—he always had and he always would have. And now she knew he'd also had her son, Hani, all this time.

She took a step forward but stopped. Amir stood only meters away, listening absently to the stream of consciousness that flowed from Hani, who was still obscured by the trees. Despite the bitterness and anger she felt towards Amir, she was struck by how different he appeared now. The change in his voice was reflected in the change in his body language. His head was tilted to one side as he listened to Hani, all attention, and his hand reached out to where the hedge obscured Hani.

This was the man she remembered. Physically he was the same, except his hair had been longer then. Now, his thick black hair was cut short—nothing could be out of control, after all. But his body, what she could see of it in the formal suit, was much the same. Despite her anger, her stomach contracted with lust at the sight of him, just as it had the moment she'd entered the room. She cleared her throat and stood tall. It made no difference. It was unimportant because their relationship was over. But her relationship with her son was about to begin, whatever Amir believed.

Then he turned to face her. His eyes narrowed against the harsh afternoon sunshine and his inscrutable expression returned as his gaze rested on her. Shadows cast by his sudden frown made his dark eyes opaque and, beneath them, the shallow cusp of his lower lid was tight. The intensity of that stare was like a reflection of his soul—dark and impenetrable. Ruby couldn't move. The very air was still, as if the late afternoon was asleep or holding its breath. What his eyes held, Ruby couldn't say. Hate? Love? There was only one thing she knew. He'd been lying. He wasn't indifferent.

The boy's laughter broke the spell. He ran out from the shelter of the trees and Ruby saw him for the first time. It was the moment she'd been waiting for, and yet it wasn't as she'd imagined. It felt unreal.

Hani's blue eyes sparkled with laughter in the sunlight as he poured water from a hose onto an elaborate maze of waterways he'd created in the sandpit. His blond hair flopped into his eyes and his tanned legs were wet from his games.

Tears sprang to her eyes as the severity of her loss hit her. The tiny baby she remembered had grown into this boy about whom she knew nothing. She repressed her tears instantly. She drew both arms across her stomach and held herself tight, not allowing any part of her to show what she really felt. Because if she broke down, she didn't know if she'd be able to pull herself together again.

Then Hani turned to her, following his father's gaze. Wide blue eyes. Her eyes. The boy turned quickly to his father.

"*Baba!* Who is this lady?"

"Hani, this is my friend, Miss Ruby Armand. Ruby, please allow me to introduce my son, Hani."

Uncertainly, Ruby stepped towards them, unable to take her eyes off Hani. He wiped his muddy hands on the back of his shorts and stepped forward with a curiously formal expression for a five-year-old. "Good morning, Miss Armand."

Ruby had to swallow a huge lump of emotion before any words could emerge. She cleared her throat. "Good morning, Hani. What is it you're making? May I see?"

"No." Amir's voice, while not loud, was commanding and Hani stopped himself from showing Ruby his game. He was obviously accustomed to doing exactly what his father demanded of him. Amir turned to Hani's nanny who hovered close by. "Hani needs to be cleaned up and then brought to the library. We'll have tea with him there."

Ruby's heart ached as Hani's face dropped.

"No," she said. All three looked at her in surprise. "I'd like to see the game."

She didn't look at Amir but reached out her hand to the little boy, half-expecting Amir to stop her at any moment. Much to her surprise, he didn't say anything, and Hani trustingly took her hand as they walked over to the sand pit. She knelt beside him, ignoring the mud that splashed onto her yellow dress.

"You see." He crouched beside her and pointed to the

trickle of water coming from a hose supported by two sticks. "I'm learning about water mills." He glanced at his father who stood behind, listening and watching intently. "Aren't I, Baba?"

"Yes. In theory. In practice you appear to be making a mess."

Ruby ignored Amir's rebuke. "And how old are you, Hani?"

"I'm five," he said proudly.

"And you're learning *so* much. When I was your age I used to like playing with water. I'd turn the hose on my friend until she was good and soaked."

Hani's shocked face would have made Ruby laugh under any other circumstances.

"Didn't your father tell you off?"

"No, he'd grab the hose and turn it on me." She sighed. "Fun times." She smiled at Hani, who was carefully digesting this startling piece of information. He stood up and twitched the hose until the deep rill along which the water flowed, flooded. He giggled.

Ruby glanced at Amir who sent her a warning frown. He opened his mouth to speak but suddenly Hani laughed and whatever Amir had been about to say was forgotten. They both turned to look at Hani. The infectious sound continued as Hani, who had placed one bare foot into the mud, brought his other foot to join it and jumped up and down, splashing mud all around. The sound of his laughter curled around her heart and nestled there. She wouldn't be leaving him. No matter what Amir said.

IT WASN'T until early evening that Hani was taken away to rest before dinner. He turned before he disappeared into the building and gave Ruby a wave. She grinned and waved back.

"He likes you."

Ruby fell into step beside Amir. "Don't sound so surprised. Some people do, you know."

"Of course. Too many people do, if the gossip columns are to be believed."

"I'm surprised you read them."

"I don't. But it's impossible to avoid your name."

"So, do you?"

"What?"

"Believe them?"

He glanced at her, a wry expression on his face. "They publish a version of the truth, but perhaps not the whole truth."

"Whenever you want to hear the true version, all you have to do is ask."

"And why would I want to do that?"

"Simple curiosity, if nothing else."

"I don't have time to indulge myself in idle curiosity. I have no need to know anything about your past. It doesn't concern me. What I need is your agreement to proceed with Hani's treatment."

Ruby covered the sinking disappointment and flutter of anxiety with her usual nonchalance. She sighed. "Life must be so simple for you."

He didn't bother to answer. "Would you like a drink? Perhaps we could sustain a civil conversation for half-an-hour to conclude business?"

"Sure. Soda water please."

She sank into the soft cushions while Amir ordered drinks from a maid who'd appeared as if by magic, and lit the lanterns on the table. He sat opposite her, the late afternoon sun deepening in color behind him, enriching the hills that lay beyond the irrigated gardens with a mellow glow. Here, in the private wing of the palace, they were secluded from the public face of the palace which fronted the city below them.

"Hani doesn't look sick. A little on the pale side, maybe, but not unduly so."

"No. It was only a routine blood test that revealed the problem. We've managed to keep him well so far. But we've no idea how long it will last. He could be fine for months—years even, but the disease can also turn suddenly. The consultant says it could happen at any time. He's currently undergoing new treatment which the Boston consultant has arranged. But we need to ensure arrangements for the blood transfusion are in place for when it's needed."

"How long have you known?"

"Not long. A few weeks."

"And you've delayed contacting me for a few weeks. I'm surprised."

"I tried other options first. I wasn't enamored with the idea of bringing you into our lives."

She bit her lip with irritation and looked away. She realized that if he'd found another solution, she wouldn't be sitting here now. She wouldn't have spent the afternoon with her son.

The maid came out with the drinks and placed them on the table between them. She took a sip from her glass, not trusting herself to speak immediately. She placed it on the table with careful deliberation.

"So." She sat back and looked at him directly. She didn't want any prevarication, any evasiveness from him. She needed to know where she stood. "What exactly will be required of me?"

"Firstly, we need your blood screened. If all is well, we need you to look after yourself. Make sure you are in the best of health and then, when the consultant names the day—sooner rather than later—you will go to hospital and give your blood to Hani."

"How nice and orderly you have it arranged. I come in, make sure I'm in the peak of health, give Hani what he needs, and then disappear."

"Not disappear. This may be ongoing. I need you to be available immediately if required."

"And I get, what?"

"You know."

"Right, a million dollars."

"Surely that's enough, even for you?"

She shook her head, unable to believe that after what they'd had together, he could think she'd be so heartless. "Why do you think I'd be so mercenary? What have I done to make you imagine that?"

He huffed. "I don't need to imagine anything. The facts speak for themselves."

"What facts? What the hell are you talking about?"

"The money I gave you for one thing."

"The money? What money?"

"Don't give me that!" He leaned forward, and looked at her, really looked for the first time since they'd met. "The money, Ruby. When you sent your friend, Caro, to me demanding money. I gave it to her and you went away."

"I what?!" She jumped up. "You think I took money from you? I haven't seen Caro since, since..." She racked her mind trying to remember. She opened her eyes wide as the memory hit her full force. "Since Hani was born."

He shrugged. "Yes. She told me she was with you at the birth."

"Yes, she was. She kept telling me that adoption was the only thing open to me. Eventually I agreed. I was sick, it

29

seemed the only option. And then...afterwards, I never saw her again."

The silence between them was tense—full of unspoken words, words they didn't dare utter.

She sat down, trying to swallow the bile at the thought of her old friend's betrayal. "Seems Caro took advantage of the situation to fleece you." Did she imagine it, or was there a crack in Amir's armor? "And you were so willing to think badly of me that you believed every word she said."

The crack in his armor immediately closed up. "It was *your* signature on the adoption forms. That was all I needed to know." He slid a card across the table. "Here's the name of the best doctor in Janub Havilah. He's expecting you. I've ordered a thorough physical."

"And no doubt it will be reported back to you."

"I see you're beginning to understand."

"My understanding you was never in question. My agreeing with you was."

He shook his head in confusion. "What are you talking about?"

"I will do as you say on one condition."

"And that is?"

"I spend time with my son. I get to know my son. I *live* with my son."

"Live with him? In what capacity?" he scoffed. "Don't be ridiculous. Nanny, teacher, nurse?"

"*Mother.*"

"That's impossible. I am not one of your loose-living friends where anything goes. I am raising Hani in a tradi- tional manner. I will marry again soon. How can I have the mother of my child living alongside my wife?"

"Do you have someone in mind?"

"That's not your concern."

"I bet you have a checklist. I wonder what's on it? 'Fertile', 'appropriately behaved', 'dutiful', 'maternal', 'beautiful', but not in a flashy way of course. Wouldn't want to frighten the establishment with too much showiness."

His lips quirked with either humor or irritation, she couldn't tell behind that cool facade. "You've described my new wife so well."

He did have someone in mind. The thought hit her in the gut. She swallowed the bile that the mere thought of Amir with another woman elicited. A woman for Amir, and a new mother for Hani. "So you *do* know her."

He shrugged. "I know her identity, but we've never met. Not that it's any of your business."

"You're so cold and calculating. You've changed so much."

"As have you."

He took a drink of his soda water but his eyes never left hers. They sat contemplating each other in silence.

She swallowed. It had to be now. There was no time to lose, not if he already had someone lined up to marry.

"I repeat. I want to live with my son."

"And I repeat. That's impossible."

"Not if you married me. Made it legal. We can co-exist easily in your vast palace without regular contact. But I *must* be with my child. You agreed to an arranged marriage once— to Mia—for your mother's and family's sake. Why not again? Why not, this time, for our son's sake?"

He shook his head. "You're amazing. You sit there and conjure up preposterous schemes like that. What is it you're really after? More money?"

She rummaged in her bag and withdrew the check. She held it up to the dying light and, in front of his eyes, tore it from top to bottom. Turned it around and tore it again. She dropped it into the lantern whose flames consumed it within seconds, before dying down once more. "I don't want your money. Get your lawyers to draw up all the pre-nups that will satisfy them. All I want is to be with my son. To make him well again and to watch him grow. For five years I've tried to find out where he was and you stopped me. You've robbed me of five years of him. I want the rest."

Amir wove his fingers tightly together and propped his elbows onto the table. He rubbed his fists across his mouth in an uncharacteristic sign of agitation. His eyes were as black as night, like smoldering coals, and as hot. "I don't believe a word you say. I think you want to be my wife for all that it would bring you—status and more money. Not Hani. You revealed your maternal feelings the day you signed the adoption papers. You signed away any rights to Hani the day you signed those papers."

"Ah, but you've created *new* rights for me, a *new* bargaining position. No doubt *that* was what you were so afraid of, *that* was why you didn't contact me immediately. And you were right. If you want me to help Hani, you *will* marry me. It's non-negotiable."

"I don't understand." The words were tense and muffled behind his hands. "Why? You don't want him. You made that plain. You gave him away, for Christ's sake."

"Listen carefully, Amir. I know you find it hard to understand anyone in a different position to yourself. But try. I was eighteen—that's young, right? I was alone—pretty stressful, you have to admit—and I was sick. Check the hospital records. No, wait. I'm sure you've already done that. So sick I nearly died. And that was just the birth. Afterwards was when it really kicked in, but you won't find any official record of that. I could have handled the physical issues, but the depression? That was something else. That was something I couldn't handle. If I'd been older, had support, who knows? But I wasn't and I was at rock bottom and I made the biggest mistake of my life. One I've regretted every moment of every single day since."

"So much so that you've had to cram your poor, sad life with material things, with people, with wild partying ever since. My heart bleeds for you."

"I don't know why I bothered explaining what happened. You have no intention of trying to understand, do you? Once you've made up your mind, that's it." She shrugged dismissively. "I don't care. It's not *you* I want. You can think whatever you like. I'm not interested. But *that* is my condition. I won't live the rest of my life knowing Hani is with you, and whether I see him or not is dependent on a whim of yours."

"I don't live my life by whims."

"You know what I mean. I won't be with him for a short time only to leave again. I'd rather leave immediately."

The sun's rays were now so low they'd become dispersed, filtered through the leaves of the graceful palms. She held her breath. Everything depended on his response.

"No! This is ridiculous." He leaned towards her. "Now you've seen Hani, I don't believe you wouldn't help him. You were always swayed by your emotions. I can see it in your eyes. You'll help him all right. And I don't need to pay, I don't need to do anything to make you."

Coolly and deliberately she stood up. She'd acted, one way or another, all her life—for photo shoots, for her family, for her friends. But now there was a hell of a lot more depending on it. But this time her performance would be all the more persuasive because Amir thought her such a cold, calculating woman. All she had to do was walk away and he'd be convinced she was the woman he believed her to be.

She placed her drink on the table. "Thanks for the drink. I won't take up any more of your time. Say *Ma Salama* to Hani for me."

Her heart pounded and her chest was so tight she could hardly breathe. But he couldn't see the expression on her face and she managed to hold it together to walk to the edge of the terrace. Still he didn't say anything. Sweat pricked her forehead. She wanted to wipe it from her face but daren't do anything that might reveal her torment. She descended the first step, then the second. It wasn't until she'd reached the bottom of the terrace steps that he called out.

"Ruby!"

She swayed on the step, hardly believing her bluff had worked. She'd walked half a dozen paces—the longest and most difficult steps she'd ever walked in her life. She'd set herself a limit of twenty paces before she'd stop, before he'd know he'd won, because he was right. She'd never turn her back on her child. It was only Amir, believing the worst of her, that had allowed her bluff to succeed.

She still didn't turn around. She couldn't risk being betrayed by the tears that had sprung up at his voice. She took a long, slow, deep breath.

"Ruby, the reason I intend to marry again isn't only political, it's also to have more children, siblings for Hani. My wife *will* also be my lover."

She swallowed, the tears suddenly drying. She turned around. His eyes were still cold and inscrutable. "Lover," she repeated faintly.

He rose and came over to her. As he came close the coldness disappeared in a heartbeat. "Lover," he repeated, brandishing the word like a weapon. "Maybe not at first but at some point it has to happen. And then?" He shrugged. "We were lovers once and we couldn't get enough of each other. I think it won't be entirely disagreeable to either of us. A purely physical, practical matter. Nothing more." Her breathing hitched in her chest as her gut tightened with desire. He stood too close, not reaching out, not touching. He didn't need to. She could feel his sexual energy as if it were a force field, but one that attacked rather than deflected. "Do you agree to that?"

"Sex in return for me being with Hani. How could I refuse? Sounds like a marriage made in heaven."

"A marriage made on earth—a practical marriage. Take it or leave it."

"If I leave it, Hani will die."

"And if you take it, Hani will live and you will live *with* him."

She summoned all the strength she could, and retracing her steps, walked over to the table where she picked up her drink once more and held it up to him in a mock toast. "To marriage—may it bring us both what we wish for."

Amir held her gaze but didn't repeat the toast. "Go back to the apartment I rented for you, make whatever personal or business arrangements you need tomorrow, and return here the following day at eleven sharp. I'll have my lawyer draft some papers for your signature."

She nodded stiffly and she suddenly realized it was going to happen. The long search for her son was over. She'd found him. She was going to be with him. But there was a price to pay—marriage to a man who despised her, a man whom she couldn't trust.

"The day after tomorrow, then." She turned and walked away without a backward glance. He'd adopted their son and put a block on her ever seeing him again. And it would have worked if it hadn't have been for a quirk of nature—their blood types. She didn't begin to understand why he didn't want a stranger's blood in Hani—it would have been easily sourced. And she wasn't interested in understanding.

She'd found her son and she was determined to never lose him again—that was all that mattered. She'd do anything for her son now. Even sleep with a man who, at this moment, she hated with every cell in her body.

CHAPTER 3

*A*t least the apartment Amir had rented for her was in the middle of the city, thought Ruby.

Dressed only in a white robe, she paused by the window which had remained open all night, allowing the noise of the cars and party-goers to keep her company all night long. She looked at the futuristic glass-fronted towers which lined the busiest street in the city. The pale pink-tinted wide road was full of luxury cars, stretch limos and taxis, all obediently adhering to the speed limit and periodically pulling over to allow high-heeled, Parisian haute couture clad women to alight and trot into one luxury branded boutique after another. It was busy during the day but it wasn't until after dark that the place really came alive. And she liked alive.

Despite the fact this apartment was three times the size of her Milan home, she preferred the blaring horns and erratic driving of the Italian cars and *motorini* which roared past her Milan apartment, and the smell of freshly-roasted meats, breads and spices which drifted up from the cafes below. It was chaotic, noisy and she could lose herself in it. But here, in this quiet, subdued apartment, full of classy, understated furniture and objets d'art, designed for minimal impact, she was in danger of finding herself again. And that she dared not do.

She dressed quickly in her favorite primary colors, and pulled on a headband as she walked to the bathroom. She caught sight of herself in the mirror but looked away. She knew the image reflected back to her wasn't the one everyone else saw. She sucked in a deep breath and quickly applied her makeup, only focusing on the specific part of her requiring attention. She didn't look at the whole. Not yet. Finally she twisted out her lipstick and smoothed it over her lips before gently pressing them together. Her signature coral lipstick completed the transformation. Only then did she release a breath.

She wasn't the image of her mother any longer. She'd been transformed into a woman whom depression could not touch.

Relieved, she scanned the apartment. Her bags were packed again. She'd traveled light, not believing she'd be able to stay long in Janub Havilah. She'd spent the previous day on the phone to Italy, to the UK and the US, to friends and her agent. It hadn't taken her long to organize her life, cancel work bookings, and let her friend Ariana, with whom she shared the apartment, know that she'd be moving on. The past few years had been perfect. Ariana had needed a rent-free apartment and Ruby had needed someone to always be there at night. Because, despite the apartment's location—in the heart of Milan, with its continual urban noise—despite the beautiful furnishings and expensive artwork, Ruby couldn't bear to be alone. And knowing Ariana and her various boyfriends were close by helped fill the emptiness, helped dull her fears.

And now everything was in place. Her ties had been, if not cut, loosened, and she was ready to go live with her son.

And Amir. Everything was in place, including a dread that ate away at the heart of her. She'd have to go to hospital and risk falling into the deep pit of despair from which it seemed impossible to climb, from which her mother had been unable to surface and which had ended her life. The ancient Greeks had a word for it—melancholia, and she had a word for it— hell. She'd be walking into the thing she most dreaded, but she had no choice because it would lead her to the thing she most valued.

The call to prayer burst upon the city from the muezzin tower in the midst of the old quarter and, startled, she turned to check the clock. It was time to go. Amir had been as precise about the time as he was with everything else. She'd got what she'd wanted. She didn't want to risk him changing his mind. She picked up her bags and cast one last look around the apartment where she'd arrived three nights earlier, summoned to see her son. She'd had no thought during that wakeful first night that she'd not only be moving in with Hani, but would also be marrying the man who'd broken her heart five years earlier.

"You're late." Amir's mood worsened at the sight of her. She was wearing a short dress of bright primary colors combined in a striking design. The loud optimism of her clothing clashed with the refined surroundings of the palace, and clashed with the fears he had for his son, fears he'd yet to tell Ruby about. How could he, when he still didn't trust her?

"Amir! So pleasant to see you, too. Meeting in the library again, appropriate place for a business meeting, I guess. A merger of sorts."

"Keep your smiles for someone they might impress. Sit down." He watched as she gracefully sat on the leather sofa—

not the hard chair he'd indicated—leaned back and crossed her long, beautiful legs. His gaze lingered there, as he was sure she'd intended. He turned without meeting her eyes, picked the papers from his desk and dropped them on the coffee table in front of her. "My lawyer has prepared the papers—a standard pre nuptial."

She raised her brow and smiled at him sweetly. "Standard? Since when has anything we do been 'standard?'"

She swept up the papers and proceeded to read through them with care. She didn't say a word and neither did Amir. It gave him a chance to watch her.

The first time he'd seen her, over six years earlier when he'd been visiting his mother's family in Italy, she'd walked into a dark bar in Milan and had literally brightened the room with the clashing colors of her clothes, her white blonde hair, and eyes that sparkled with fun. After a life of responsibility and duty, he'd been attracted to her like a moth that had lived too long in darkness. It was the same now, he mused. She seemed brighter if anything. Perhaps a little too bright.

She lifted her eyes suddenly to his and caught him looking at her. Yes, the eyes looked brighter, harder, more guarded. His own eyes narrowed in response. "Everything as you expected?"

"Sure." She grabbed the pen and signed it with a flourish. "More than I expected. It's a generous settlement you'll give me if we divorce."

"*When* we divorce."

"So certain."

"Of you? Yes." Of course he was. She had no idea how closely he'd watched her life over the past five years.

"Like you know me so well," she said, her facetious tone grating.

He smiled. "You're not difficult to know. A brief friendship—"

"Friendship?"

"Followed by a predictable career in the limelight."

She sighed, sat back and crossed her legs once more. "How comforting it must be to be so wise, to know so much about everyone and everything."

"Not comforting. Quite *dis*comforting in fact."

"Because people don't meet your high standards?"

"Indeed. It rarely happens."

"Perhaps you expect too much."

"Of you, quite possibly." He pushed the papers away.

She cocked her head to one side, her lips and eyes tight with irritation. "You know, you remind me of something. I know! You're like the barriers which protect Venice from flooding—untouched by the pounding chaos of the sea, refusing it entry to your hallowed grounds."

"Strong, you mean. Protective of things and people I hold dear."

"Hard and unfeeling is what I mean."

He rose. "Thank you for sharing the product of your over-active imagination. Most enlightening. Now we've concluded our business, you may wish to settle in."

Ruby didn't move. "You're quite wrong, you know."

He frowned. "About anything in particular? Or"—he shrugged—"simply everything?"

"The divorce. I don't intend to divorce and you won't either." She leaned forward. "I've only just found him again and I won't be leaving. I'll make him well, and I'll make him happy."

"You'll make him well, certainly. And as for happy? He's happy already, as am I." He ignored her laughter. "I need nothing further from you." He ground his teeth as he watched her laughter subside. If only she'd taken the million dollars.

"Talking of Hani," Ruby continued, as if she'd somehow won the argument. "How is he today? Where can I find him?"

It seemed she was happy to ignore anything she didn't want to think about. Either that or she was deliberately trying to goad him. There was nothing for it; he'd have to show her who was in control here in no uncertain terms.

"You can't. He's not feeling well. I've given instructions for him not to be disturbed."

"But I can—"

"No, you can't. He's easily excited."

"Not like you then."

"Not in that way, certainly. More like what little I know of his birth mother, I would say."

She raised a perfectly arched eyebrow. "Would you?"

"Certainly. You can't keep away from people. You are always where a photographer is close by. Always acquiring people, things, money. Never alone."

"I share my apartment with friends. How is that a crime? And I'm not promiscuous, not that that's any business of yours."

"I'd assumed my sources had failed me when they said you always returned to your bed alone."

She huffed. "Your sources! What are you? Some sort of a Machiavelli?"

"He was a distant relation of my mother's."

Her laughter filled the room. He'd forgotten her laugh, hadn't realized she had the same infectious laugh as Hani, and it drove deep inside, bypassing the hurt, the anger, the pain, arriving at a place he didn't believe still existed. He smiled, despite himself.

She looked at him and stopped laughing instantly. "Figures."

He was suddenly aware of the connection, and stood up and looked around, needing to break it. He walked to his desk and pressed a silent buzzer. "My housekeeper will show you to your room."

"Just one more thing. When will we marry?"

"Not immediately. There are things I need to sort out with the other... negotiations first."

She nodded, looked down at the ridiculously high sandals she wore and shuffled a foot slightly. He frowned. For one moment, when she looked up, he could have sworn the brilliant blue of her eyes was clouded with sadness. Then his housekeeper entered the room and the cloud passed over. "Of course."

She followed the housekeeper out the door and didn't turn back.

THE HOUSEKEEPER STOPPED outside a pair of double doors. To the right was another pair of doors. "This is my room?" Ruby asked.

"Yes, madam."

"And here?" Ruby pointed to the other door.

"His Majesty's suite."

Of course. Right next to hers. What she wouldn't have given for such a set-up five years ago. But now? Right now she hated him.

But at least she wouldn't be on her own. There would be someone close beside her. The palace was vast, and all the activity and business side of the palace was far away from here. She hated to be alone, hated the quiet. She entered the room and looked around, aware of the retreating steps of the housekeeper, leaving her alone. She closed her eyes. There was nothing but silence.

She paced the room as panic began to set in, because it

wasn't just the loss of Hani that haunted her. She closed her eyes tight shut and pressed the palm of her hand to her forehead, pushing it around in a circle, trying to stave off the panic.

She'd have to go to a hospital again. The last time had been when she'd given birth to Hani. It had been a difficult birth but nothing like what had happened afterwards. She hadn't even seen the depression coming—the same depression that had dogged her mother, until she'd taken her life. It was the ever-present fear that she'd succumb to the 'black dog' that scared her.

But she wouldn't think of that today. She was good at evasive thoughts. She was good at tucking away her fears, drowning them in activity. She unpacked her bag and tidied all her possessions away.

Then she picked up her hairbrush and pounded it against her head. But looking into the mirror she could see the fear in her eyes. She continued to brush her hair as she strode to the windows, opened them and leaned out. Her room looked out onto the palace's private gardens enclosed in a high wall and trees, beyond which lay the mountains and desert of the other lands of Havilah. Sunlight filtered through the trees, softening the harsh white walls, casting shadows across the rectangular pond which ran the length of the courtyard. It was a peaceful view, an empty view and one she didn't want. What she wanted was to see Hani. Alone.

She'd signed the papers, just as Amir had wanted; she was in her room, just as he wanted. But she couldn't see Hani. She didn't even know where his bedroom was in this vast palace. She tossed the brush on to the bed. She didn't know, but Amir's staff would.

～

IT WAS LATE. Ruby lay in her bed waiting for the last sounds of activity to die down. She didn't want to be discovered walking around the silent palace, as Amir's staff had warned her that she'd likely be turned back to her room. His staff had soon opened up to her, relieved, no doubt, to find someone human in their midst. And, from what they described, it sounded as if Amir had given instructions that her every move be watched. She was more under house arrest than honored guest. It didn't help her feelings of anxiety.

She tensed at the silence that lay around her, only relaxing when she heard Amir move around in the dressing room that lay between their rooms. For one brief moment she thought he might come to her through the connecting door. Then he moved away, back into his bedroom and she exhaled slowly. Her hand crept over her stomach as she remembered all the times he'd come to her in the small bed-sit in Milan, when they had no thought of anything in the world, except love. There would have been no hesitation then—he would have known what she wanted. But now, for all his surveillance of her, he didn't know her at all. All he knew was she wanted to be with her son. And he was with-holding even that from her.

She turned over, the sheets twisting around her body, and looked out across the beautiful dark hills which separated the coastal strip where the city had been built, from the inland desert. She'd never been to the desert, but Amir used to talk about it. She'd been entranced at the faraway look which had come into his eyes when he'd described the desert at night, the magic of it, the colors of the sky, the sound of the music the Bedouin played. It had been the last step to falling in love with him.

The lust had been instant, but she'd clung as long as she could to the idea that their relationship was a casual thing, something which would be over after the summer, when he returned to his home in Havilah. Of course, she hadn't known that his family happened to be royal. But she doubted whether that would have been enough to stop the free-fall into the depths of love with him. Once there, there'd been no way back. And then she'd fallen pregnant and everything had changed.

Hani, her son. The baby she'd thought she'd lost forever was only a corridor away from her. Her mind was filled with her son's face, surrounded by the mop of blond hair, and she felt an urgent need to see him as a mother would, asleep in his bed. She rose and pulled on her white silk robe.

She left her bedroom and softly padded along the hushed corridor to the nursery wing, the solid stone walls and price-less rugs effectively absorbing any sound.

She opened the door quietly and stood, waiting for her eyes to become accustomed to the dark. She didn't see him at first.

Moonlight revealed mobiles of airplanes engaged in battle, toy cars tidily parked beside a racetrack and a model railway, whose engines were carefully placed in the sidings. She smiled. Tidiness wasn't something he'd inherited from her. Her smile faded. She knew so little about Amir. Their brief summer affair had ended before it had begun. But the consequences had been anything but brief.

She took another step into the room and stopped abruptly.

Thick blond curly hair framed a face relaxed in sleep; arms were flung wide either side of his head; legs stuck out between twisted, white sheets. The only sounds were his rhythmic breathing, the ticking of a clock and the soft thud of her heart.

She didn't know how long she stood: watching, absorb-ing, wanting. But awe soon gave way to pain as she thought of the years she'd missed seeing him. She screwed up her eyes and pinched her nose, trying to stop the tears, but they came anyway.

"A beautiful sight, isn't he?"

Amir's whispered words sent a shiver down her spine and she turned with a sob. He stood beyond the fall of light, his face like a crude charcoal drawing. The faint traces of moonlight were unable to reveal any subtlety of expression, only broad strokes of dark and shade.

"Amir!" she whispered, hating how vulnerable she felt. She swept her thumbs under her eyes, trying to rub away the traces of tears. "Come to throw me out?"

"And why would I do that?" His voice, too, was soft so as not to disturb Hani.

He stepped closer to her, moving into the dim light. His white shirt hung unbuttoned over his dark trousers and a sprinkling of hair trailed down his muscled stomach and lower. She looked up sharply and frowned. His eyes, too, were undone.

She shrugged. "I don't know? Perhaps there's something in the pre-nup about me not visiting my son after dark?"

"You always were irrational."

She smiled tightly. "I seem to remember you call anyone irrational who disagrees with you."

His lips quirked into a glimmer of a smile. "I do, because it's true. I'm here because I was curious to see where you were going."

"To see Hani, of course. Try to make up for lost time."

"You'll never do that. But that was your decision."

"And it makes it all the more bitter."

He stepped closer to her, so close she could feel his breath against her cheek. She folded her arms, as much in an effort to stop herself shaking as to block him. He reached out with his hand and she closed her eyes briefly, not knowing what to expect but only knowing that to move would show weakness.

He turned her face to his and pushed her hair away. "You're paler than you appear in your photos."

She tried to move away but something held her fast. She closed her eyes to stop herself becoming lost in his dark eyes. But instead she became more acutely aware of his touch on her face, of the effect of his presence on her body. "Photographers' magic," she whispered. "People change in five years."

"Not you, not so much." His thumb scarcely touched her bottom lip as it swept across it.

She opened her eyes as he dipped his head close to hers. His frown deepened briefly—revealing a flicker of some emotion that broke through the dispassionate control—but it was gone before she could identify it.

"I wish I could return the compliment," she whispered.

"It's not a compliment. You obviously receive so few that you mistake it for one. If I were to say that your hair"—he picked up a strand and pulled it between his thumb and forefinger—"had the texture of silk and was the color of white gold in the moonlight..."

Her breath tightened in her throat as she held herself still, all her senses concentrated on the drag of his fingers through her hair.

"That," he continued, "would be a compliment."

She gripped his hand in an effort to stop its motion down her hair to her neck. But, instead, the shivers of sensation intensified as he gained control of her hand and she felt the pressure of his thumb against her skin.

"But you've lost weight." His tone of voice became softer. "Too much modeling, too much partying, not enough food. And that"—he raised her chin, forcing her to face him—"is not a compliment."

"It's my reality," she whispered, trying to control the

bedlam of emotions that his words and his touch stirred deep within. "It has nothing to do with you."

His mouth twisted slightly and he lowered his eyes for the first time. "You are, of course, correct. But he is." He nodded his head in the direction of their son, Hani, still soundly asleep. She followed his gaze, drinking in the details of her son—covers half-kicked off, long, lean limbs tangled in the sheets. He was the image of a secure, cared-for boy—peaceful in his own home. She tore her eyes away, trying to suppress the pain of those missed years. She swallowed a sob.

"Seen enough?" His generous lips had relaxed from the straight line of tension she'd seen earlier into a shadow of a smile.

"I'll never see enough. And you know it."

"Good. It will make it easier for you to do what you have to do." He dipped his head still further. "Come." The single word conjured images of seduction in her mind. "Leave Hani to sleep. He needs it." His hand trailed down her arm until he grasped her hand and pulled her out of the room.

She was scarcely aware of her surroundings—the ornate-gilded frames of paintings of desert landscapes, of bowls of fruit, of long-dead people, pictures devoid of life—as they walked along the corridor. All her senses were focused on the pressure of his hand over hers. She should pull her hand away but there was comfort in that firm grip and there was a commanding sexuality which made the years roll away to when they'd first met. He stopped at his door, glanced down at their joined hands and looked into her eyes. But he didn't speak and she had no clue as to his thoughts.

"Do you remember, Amir, when we first met?"

He didn't say a word. There was no movement of his head to give himself away. She refused to be intimidated. She had to make him try to remember, try to regain some connection, if they were to be together for the sake of their little boy. She had to breathe some life into this place, into this relationship, if they were to have any chance of making a success of this, for Hani's sake.

She swallowed. "I was in the market haggling with a store-holder over the price of plums."

She could see the memory spark something in him.

"You had no money. I don't know how you lived."

"And you gave him the money and I took the bag."

"And you offered me a plum," he said, his voice a shade softer.

"And you took it, and finished it much later, in bed." She shook her head. "It was the first time I'd ever done anything like that. The first, and the last."

"We were young." He let go of her hand and opened his door. "Goodnight, Ruby."

She watched him close it behind him. "And in love," she added, before going into her own bedroom and closing the door. She lay on the bed and looked up at the ornate plaster ceiling, forcing herself to acknowledge that she might marry Amir, that he might not be completely indifferent to her, but there was no way he'd ever allow himself to feel anything for her again.

CHAPTER 4

*R*uby was awakened the next morning by her phone ringing. She looked around in a daze, squinting in the bright sunlight from between the curtains which she'd opened in the night. When she couldn't sleep, she needed to see outside, to see lights around her, to know she wasn't alone. Unfortunately, the palace had been built above the city and behind it lay the empty hills. So, instead, she had to make do with the solar lights which edged the pond below, and the sound of the water splashing from the spout at the end and the trickle as it flowed from the pond into a rill, which traced a pattern down to a lower garden. But now the sun was bright and she realized she'd slept in.

She grabbed her phone from the bedside table and peered at it. "*Si?*" she replied out of habit. She listened for a few moments to Amir informing her she'd overslept, before she tried to speak, only to be spoken over by him. She looked at her phone as he continued to speak, and then finished the call while he was in mid flow, and pulled the covers over her. She never rose before nine. Between her work and partying, she rarely got to bed before two and she had no idea what anything before ten o'clock looked like.

She'd just about fallen into a doze when there was a sharp rapping at the door. She ignored it. Unfortunately it didn't cease. She rose and opened it.

Standing at the door was a very smart middle-aged woman with a laptop under her arm. "Miss Armand?"

"*Si?*" Ruby was acutely aware that she was wearing a flimsy silk nightdress. She pulled a robe from the back of the door and hauled it on. "And you are?"

The woman stuck out a hand, devoid of rings, but with a perfect clear manicure. "Madame Simone Beaumont. His Majesty has assigned me to you."

Despite her irritation at being assigned someone without consultation, she couldn't help but smile at how predictable Amir was. "Of course he has," she said with a grin. "Come in." Ruby stood aside and the woman walked to the desk. "You'll have to excuse me," continued Ruby. "I'm not used to getting up this early."

"*D'accord*," Simone said as she set up her laptop. "His Majesty advised me that you might not be, shall we say, 'on board', initially."

As a model Ruby was used to being half-dressed in front of people, and wasn't embarrassed, unlike, apparently, Simone, who kept her eyes fixed on the computer.

"I'd have been more 'on board' if he'd told me about it." She waved her hand dismissively. "Anyhow, it doesn't matter. What does matter is that I need a coffee. I'll go and get one, then maybe we can do whatever it is you want me to do."

But before Ruby could pick up the phone, there was a knock at the door. Simone opened it and a maid entered with a breakfast tray. Ruby raised an eyebrow. "Seems you've anticipated my needs."

"That's what I'm paid for, Miss Armand."

"Please, if you're going to anticipate everything I need, at least call me 'Ruby'." Ruby grinned and, for the first time since the woman had entered the room, they made eye contact. Simone smiled hesitantly.

"Thank you, but—"

"I insist. It has to be 'Ruby'. I don't answer to anything else." Except "mama" she thought, and it was too early to even hope for that epithet.

"Ruby," said Simone, as if she were trying out a strange word.

Ruby poured two coffees and gave one to Simone, who looked briefly startled. "I bet you don't often get to call people by their first name since you've been working for Amir." She took a sip of coffee. "How long have you worked for him?"

"Only two months. Since he arranged for you to stay here."

Ruby's good humor suddenly evaporated. Amir had planned this whole thing down to the last detail, without her knowing any of it. She took another sip of coffee and placed it on the tray, ignoring the rest of the food. "Seems Amir has everything under control."

"Oh, yes, madam, I mean Ruby, he does. He leaves nothing to chance." She flicked through the laptop. "I've done extensive research about your optimum diet and have appointments arranged for you for tests and so on. If you'd like to take a look?"

Ruby took a deep breath and rose. "What I'd like is to get dressed, Simone. May I call you Simone?"

Simone looked anxious. "Of course. But I'm sorry, madam, Ruby, if I have offended, but—"

Ruby couldn't help think being called 'Madam Ruby' was worse than Miss Armand, but it was too late now. It made her sound like the owner of a brothel.

"No, really. You haven't done anything. It's what you've been employed to do which irks me. I'm sure your arrangements have been faultless, and I'm sure I'll get used to the idea, eventually."

"Thank you. That would certainly make things easier."

"So, unless you'd like to shower me, too, maybe we could meet up a little later and go through the schedule?"

Simone jumped up. "Of course, madam, I mean Ruby. Would an hour's time be convenient?"

"It would," said Ruby, with a smile. She was used to working with people who tried to organize her, both at the model agency and at photographic shoots, and she appreciated their work. She also appreciated the fact that the woman was no doubt brilliant at her job and not to blame for being hired. The blame for that lay squarely with Amir. It wasn't in Ruby's nature to make enemies, and she always seemed to empathize with people too much, even if she wanted to be angry with them. There was only one person she had no empathy with at the moment, and that was Amir, who'd planned everything with military precision.

Simone smiled with relief again. "Shall I return to your room?"

"No, thanks. How about we meet outside on the terrace, and we can have a chat and make things as easy as possible for both of us?"

Simone's smiled widened. She'd obviously been told to expect Ruby to be obstinate and awkward, but that wasn't Ruby's way. She'd always found that relaxing people, putting them at their ease and listening to them, was both easier and, ultimately, more effective.

Ruby went into the bathroom, turned on the shower and thought of Hani. It was all for him. The only reason she was here was to have a relationship with Hani. And to do that, she needed to keep Simone onside, because Ruby knew what

Simone didn't—the last thing Amir would want was for Ruby to spend time with Hani, so his aim was to keep her busy and away from her son. Ruby grinned to herself. Pity Amir didn't know people as well as she did. With his staff as her allies, she'd make sure she was one step ahead of any plans Amir had for her.

～

AMIR TURNED off the phone in disgust and looked out the window of the private jet. They'd be landing at his palace soon. He was returning from a meeting with the two other kings of Havilah, updating them on the sudden change in his plans. They worked closely together. They had to, for the safety of their countries, and any changes—personal or otherwise—were always communicated to them in person. Despite the fact his decision would mean the task of marriage to the Tawazun sheikha would fall on one of the others, they'd congratulated him. But he'd never felt less like being congratulated. Ruby was turning his world upside down.

Instead of returning to his home, he was returning to a battleground. And it seemed, after listening to the new assistant he'd hired to keep Ruby in order, that Ruby was winning the battle.

Instead of a day filled with back-to-back meetings concerning her health and diet, she'd only attended one hospital appointment and had spent the rest of the day with Hani. That was most certainly not Amir's intention. And nor was it his intention for his own staff to have allowed such a thing, especially when they'd received express instructions to the contrary.

"We're about to land, your majesty," said the air steward.

Amir nodded, and shifted his seat upright and clipped on

his belt. He looked around the small cabin, which was still full of reminders of his dead wife. Photos of the three of them: him, Mia and Hani—picture perfect in different cities around the world—were grouped around the tastefully decorated cabin. All the work of Mia.

She'd been as organized as him and had been a superb mother to Hani, despite the facts surrounding Hani's birth, of which he'd made her fully aware. She'd been a clever woman, an ambitious woman, and an unemotional one. She'd been a perfect hostess, and wife and mother. But she was dead, from a head-on collision with a drunk driver, and nothing could bring her back. But he refused to believe that the order they'd created in their life was also gone.

The plane landed on the tarmac with deft precision and Amir closed his eyes for a few moments. He opened them again as the plane slowed to a halt. He waited for the seatbelt sign to dim, and flicked off the belt. No, he'd not allow the chaos into his life; life needed order—without that, there was nothing.

"WHAT THE HELL?" came a gruff voice at the door.

Hani and Ruby turned around at the same time and burst out laughing. The sight of Amir, standing in a doorway with streamers flowing all around him, dislodging a balloon, was so ridiculous that even his assistant, Jamal, had to work hard to prevent a grin. He carefully put down the egg and spoon which he and Simone had been balancing, as they'd raced Hani and Ruby across the large room to a finish line by the door, festooned with ribbons.

Amir batted a balloon out of his way, which had the gall to waft in front of him. "Is someone going to tell me what the hell's going on here?"

Ruby was aware of the flinch in Hani's narrow shoulders under her hands, at Amir's words. She felt a flash of unusual anger. "Amir! Come in and join the fun!"

"Fun? You call this fun?"

She gave Hani's shoulders one more squeeze before going over to Amir, whose narrowed eyes were fixed on her, daring her to bridge the distance between them, challenging her to confirm that what they were having was, indeed, "fun".

She accepted the implicit challenge and stepped right up to him, invading his space, refusing to be cowed by his aggressive stance. She glanced around at the others with a forced smile. "Hani, why don't you go with Jamal and Simone and get ready for dinner?"

The three of them didn't need asking twice and they disappeared amid a bloom of soapy bubbles, which were being pumped from a small toy machine that Ruby had had delivered when she'd discovered that Hani had never blown bubbles before.

At least Amir had sufficient feeling for his son to restrain himself until Jamal had closed the door behind them.

She turned to face him, arms crossed. She refused to flinch under his black, angry stare.

"*Now* are you going to tell me what the hell is going on?" He grimaced and paced away, as if being close to her pained him. He swiveled on his heels, his hands thrust into his pockets, but she could see they were balled into fists. He was as tense as a drum and about as likely to be quiet. All it needed was for her to tap the taut surface and it would explode. Well, she thought, why not?

"I'm giving my son a taste of fun." She wondered which would be the trigger words. "My son", or "fun". Both, by the looks of things.

Amir's complexion reddened. Unusual, she thought, that his face should go so bright, while his eyes darkened. But the drum still hadn't sounded. She decided to opt for the "fun" word to press home her advantage.

"Fun," she added with emphasis, "which seems to have been spectacularly missing from his life so far."

He grunted and turned around once more. She decided it was probably the 'spectacularly' word which got him that time. When he turned around he could barely contain his rage. "You walk into Hani's life out of the blue—"

"Only because you've only just told me about him—"

"And decide that we're not raising him properly. That takes some—"

"We? Who is we?"

He lowered his brow. "You know full well I mean my wife and I."

"It's only *you* now. And you're not doing a good job." She pointed to where Hani had left the room. "That boy was scared when you entered the room and started carrying on."

"I was not carrying on, I was—"

"He was scared! He was trembling under my hands."

He looked slightly chastened. "And whose fault was that?" He batted away another balloon. "If you hadn't turned our home into a... a *carnival* site, then I wouldn't have been angry."

"It's not a carnival. It's a party. It seems he didn't have the first idea about what a real kid's party was like, so I thought I'd show him."

Amir was silent as he looked at her. A muscle flickered in his jaw as he struggled to deal with what she was saying. It was always best to take advantage of silence, Ruby felt. It was like a vacuum and could be easily filled and taken over otherwise.

She walked to the window. "And," she added for good measure, flinging back the window and beckoning him forward. "We've been playing on the bouncy castle this afternoon. I hope that doesn't injure your sense of dignity, too."

He closed his eyes briefly in dismay before walking over to her and looking out at the bright orange and blue inflatable toy, the size of a double garage, which had been pinned to the immaculate grass by dozens of tent pegs.

She heard him swear under his breath before turning away.

"You see—"

"I've seen quite enough."

And, she thought, he probably had. She could tell she'd got through to him and that, at some level, he'd understood.

"Good." She closed the window and turned back to him. He still had his hands in his trousers, but his fists were no longer balled with rage, and his stance wasn't so aggressive. In fact when he pressed his lips together, Ruby couldn't tell if he were simply suppressing further conversation, of which he'd obviously had enough, or preventing something like a smile.

He plucked a ribbon from the string of paper chains which she and Hani had made in the morning and strung around the formal drawing room. He glanced at her and, for a minute, she thought she saw the man she'd first met. There was a glint of humor, a wicked charm which shot out of nowhere and struck at the heart of her. She needed support, and leaned back against one of the twenty Louise Quinze chairs which surrounded the over-sized mahogany table. It banged against the wood of the table and the glint in his eyes sharpened. He walked toward her and she knew that whatever advantage she'd initially gained had disappeared with her show of weakness—weakness at what those eyes could still do to her.

He stood in front of her, crowding her personal space, just as she'd crowded his earlier, and reached out to her face.

She gasped and held her breath, wondering what he was going to do. She should have moved. The Ruby her friends knew would have grabbed his hand as it reached out and taken it and turned it into whatever she wanted, but it seemed the old Ruby was nowhere to be found.

The air thickened around them, the breeze from the open doors and windows dropped, and she suddenly felt hot. His eyes narrowed once more, his lips turned into a knowing smile, as he reached into her hair and plucked out a streamer.

"You know," he said, his voice deeper, sexier and somehow far more dangerous than when he was angry. "You would have sounded far more convincing if you hadn't had the remains of these in your hair." He held up a bundle of small, sticky streamers which had issued forth from a streamer popper.

She licked her lips. "I *was* convincing, otherwise you'd still be angry."

"What makes you think I'm not?"

"The way you're looking at me."

"And what way is that? Tell me, because I'd like to hear it from those lips." He dragged the tip of his finger gently along her bottom lip, pulling it open slightly. She suddenly felt a mischievous impulse to bite his finger, but, as quickly as the thought came, his eyes changed and he withdrew it. It seemed he could read her, too.

"You're looking at me as if you want me," she said.

He stilled, his expression no longer angry or humorous, but serious. "Ruby. Don't you realize yet? I've always wanted you." Then he raised an eyebrow. "But"—he shrugged—"maybe I'm lying, like you seem to think I do. What's the lie, hey, Ruby? Me wanting you, or me not wanting you?"

She moved awkwardly away. "I don't know. I don't pretend to know you."

"Then maybe you'll understand actions rather than

words." He took her hand, pulled her to him, and kissed her firmly on the lips.

Time stood still. She was aware of nothing but the heat and power of his lips on hers, of the thudding of her heart, and the melting deep inside her. Then he pulled away, too soon. "So, now do you know?"

She nodded and put her hand against her mouth, as if she'd been burned, unable to believe what had happened. She licked her lips, tried to taste his lips once more, but the kiss had been tantalizingly brief. "Yes, I know."

"Good. Then maybe you'll tell me," he said, in a softer, huskier tone.

She shook her head. She couldn't go there. Not yet.

He sighed, and walked to the door. "I'm going to get changed, and I suggest you do the same."

"Why? Where are we going?"

"If Hani has just had a party, then I think the least that can happen is for his father to also enjoy some of the celebrations. There's a theme park near here that he mentioned once. We've never been there, but now maybe's a good time to go."

She'd scored! She took a deep breath. She'd show him that she could be gracious in victory. "I'm sure he'll love that. But he's tired now."

Amir looked concerned. "Of course. I almost forgot."

Ruby wished she hadn't said anything because the Amir she'd known so many years ago had disappeared again under the cares and concerns of the new one. But there was no way around it. Hani would be too tired for such an excursion.

"Of course," he said again, turning. "It was a silly idea."

"No, no it wasn't. And I have another one that I think he would also enjoy."

Ruby's heart leaped at the look of trust and interest which Amir gave her. "And what is that?" he asked quietly.

"He wants to eat an ice-cream from a street vendor on the river bank."

Amir nodded slowly. "I'll have to check with his dietician."

"No need. I've checked already. It's fine."

"Ice-creams it is, then."

Ruby watched Amir walk along the stone-flagged hallway, his hands thrust in his pockets, in that habitual stance of his, but his gait was easier somehow.

IT WAS GETTING dark by the time they returned. Hani had had a ball and Amir had been uncharacteristically relaxed, and had allowed Hani and Ruby to take the lead. He'd even appeared to enjoy the ice cream.

As usual Amir led them through the rear of the palace to the private wing and grounds, away from all the busyness of the administrative and ceremonial center.

They paused on the terrace and said goodnight to Hani. After a promise by Ruby to come along later and tuck him in, Amir and Ruby watched Hani disappear inside. Ruby turned with a sigh of contentment and looked out across the city to the sea, an indigo blue against a sapphire sky. It was the perfect time of day. The light lent a mystery to the already exotic landscape, diffusing and smudging the edges to make it look even romantic and mysterious. She glanced at Amir who, too, seemed to have been touched by the atmosphere.

He looked at her. "Hungry?"

"What, after that ice-cream and half of Hani's?" She laughed.

"I'm not sure Hani had much say in your eating it. You teased him a lot."

She was serious now. "You think I shouldn't have?"

"I didn't say that."

"Then what did you say?"

"I think what I'm trying to say is that Hani had a good time. And that I also had a good time."

"I did too," she said softly.

"Would you care for a drink? Here, with me?"

She nodded. She would, indeed, care. More than she could say, more than she wanted him to know.

He raised his hand and beckoned one of his staff, who were never far away. A few words and it was done.

She took a seat. "I hope I don't have to pay for these, too."

"Ah, I apologize for that. I usually have people with me to buy such things…"

"As ice creams?"

"No, that is a first."

"You should have money though, Amir. Seriously. What kind of world is Hani going to grow up in? One that he expects someone to jump up and pay for things? That's not how it works."

"It's how my world works. And my world will be his, one day."

"He needs to know how people live in the real world, Amir. To understand people."

"*I* understand people."

"No, you don't. All you do is tell people what to do, and they do it."

"Everyone except you, it seems."

"There's a reason for that, Amir."

"Because you're contrary, you're impetuous, and you're impulsive?"

"I'm all of those things. And… I'm also scared."

The pulse of the evening deepened, as their gaze fixed and became as impenetrable as the darkening dusk. "Scared?" His voice was low with disbelief.

"Yes, of course, scared. That's what one feels when something one has wanted for so long is held up before one, like bait, like it's close and yet could be yanked away at any time. I'm scared I'll lose him again."

As the silence lengthened, Ruby wasn't sure that Amir had heard, let alone understood. The drinks came and he took a sip, then placed it deliberately on the table and turned to her. The dusk was deepening with each passing moment, settling an almost violet hue over the world. Lights flared around the terrace as Amir's housekeeper turned them on. It was like a film set, with Amir taking center stage: all eyes on him—hers at least—waiting to hear him deliver the sentence which could give her a future, or take it away.

"You lost him once because you wished to. You won't lose him again unless you wish to, also."

"That won't ever happen."

"Then you have nothing to fear."

Nothing to fear... His words repeated in her head as she thought of all the things she was afraid of. Of being alone, and of the depression which had landed on her like a dark fog after Hani's birth.

"Right," she said. "Right." Then she looked into his eyes, which were growing more indistinct in the dying light. "I wish I could believe that."

He leaned forward and took her hand. "You have my word."

And, in that moment, she believed him.

"But in return, I wish you to work with Simone. The things I wish you to do around your diet and health aren't a result of any whim on my part. They're for your health, and in turn, Hani's. And yet she tells me you refused to look at your diary, or discuss your commitments which have been planned for you over the coming months."

"That's true. I wanted today with Hani. I've waited five

years for this moment. Did you really believe I was going to stay in an office doing paperwork when I could be in his company?"

"Strangely, yes, I did. I was wrong, of course. I'd underestimated your determination."

"And overestimated your ability to control me."

"No, I haven't done that. I've allowed you your day with Hani. But if you want that to continue you have to do things by the book—*my* book. And that means making sure you are fit and well and prepared for... whatever may happen."

She swallowed. Somehow she was always able to push unpleasant ideas out of her mind. And she'd done just that today, being in the moment with Hani. But it hadn't gone away. "Of course. Do you know when Hani might need the transfusion?"

"No. It will happen only if it's absolutely necessary. At the moment we're focusing on the treatment he's receiving from the consultant in Boston. She's doing some cutting edge research which could help Hani."

"So he might not need my blood? You didn't say that before."

"I wanted to make sure you agreed to the plan. I need you here as insurance for Hani."

She slid her hand out of his grip. The light had literally and figuratively gone out of the day. The brightness had been eclipsed by the fact that she was simply a tick on a form to Amir. She should have known, she shouldn't have cared, but she did. She tried to smile, to take his comment casually. "Insurance—check." She flashed him a brief, brittle smile. "I feel as if I've been reduced to an item on a form... a tick in a checkbox... a policy."

He sat back in his chair and shrugged. "You can call it whatever you like, but insurance is what you are."

She couldn't contain the hurt anymore. "Is that all you think I am?"

"It is all that matters." He paused. "That, and also the fact that you will be my wife."

"Ah, of course," she said, not bothering to keep the bitterness from her tone. "Another box checked."

He frowned. "You didn't think it was anything else, did you?"

"Of course not! And, tell me, when exactly is this 'marriage' box going to be checked?"

"There are meetings I need to have first. We'll make arrangements once they're out of the way. I'll inform you through your secretary. In the meantime"—Amir rose from his chair—"your days will be mapped out for you as per your diary. I suggest you look at it. Now, I will leave you. I have work to do, work which should have been done this afternoon. Goodnight."

As Amir walked away, he felt Ruby's eyes fixed on his back, like a homing device. It had taken all his willpower and control—of which he'd always thought he had plenty—to not look back and beckon her to come with him. Today she'd shown what she could give Hani and he was pleased about that. But it had also shown how she could single-handedly destroy his world and everything he'd worked hard to create, and worked hard to control—including his own heart. And he was anything *but* pleased about that.

CHAPTER 5

*A*t least, Ruby thought to herself, as she finished applying mascara and scrutinized the effect in the mirror, she'd been able to maintain some contact with Hani over the past week. Even if it had been only for a few hours in the late afternoon, when both their strict regimes were over for the day. Because Ruby had succumbed to Amir's control, understanding that if she wanted a relationship with Hani, she had to do as Amir said.

The date of the wedding had come sooner than she'd imagined. The secular wedding was to be private, a mere formality, nothing like the kind of wedding Amir had had with Mia, which had been a proclamation to the world of the union. This was the opposite of that—a grudging gesture. Necessary but unwanted.

She tried not to care. It was hardly the stuff of fairy tales but it secured her future with Hani—at least in the short term. At least until Amir decided she was no longer needed as 'insurance' and tired of her. But it also brought with it the prospect of intimacy with Amir. Her shaking hand accidentally dabbed dark blue mascara onto her pale cheek. She cursed under her breath as she wiped it away and stepped back from the mirror.

She wore a long-sleeved red dress which fit like a glove. Its design was demure, but its cut and fit weren't. She'd do as he requested, but only up to a point, the point when he began to encroach on her personality. There was no way she was going to allow him to dominate her. He'd already forbidden a group of her model friends to attend the ceremony. They were on a fashion shoot in the city, no doubt set up partly out of curiosity to see where Ruby had disappeared to, but she'd hardly seen them since they'd arrived. She'd had to give in to Amir on that point, but he needed to know she was still her own woman.

A knock on the door was quickly followed by the entrance of Simone, who'd rapidly become an ally in this game, albeit an amazingly discreet one.

"It's time, Ruby," she said, with a sympathetic smile.

"Thanks. Is everything in place?"

Simone blushed. "Yes, but..." She hesitated. "The dress..."

"Don't worry about it. If Amir is angry, he'll be angry with me, no one else."

Simone nodded, but looked extremely uncomfortable. Not for the first time, Ruby wondered if she was going too far, but she dismissed the idea. She'd done everything by the book this past week—been poked, prodded, and pricked for blood tests—so the least Amir could do was to be reminded that Ruby was still Ruby and that going forward their life would also be on her terms.

"Okay, let's go." She took the small posy of blood-red roses from Simone and slipped on her scarlet stiletto heels.

AMIR GLANCED AT HIS WATCH. She was late. Of course she was. Despite the fact she only had to walk from one side of the palace to the other, she was late. Just as well he'd decided to make the wedding as low key as he could by having the briefest of western style weddings. Only the celebrant, a few of his staff and Hani were in attendance. Her lateness at anything more public would have been an embarrassment.

"I have confirmation she's left her suite," he said, by way of explanation to the marriage celebrant, who'd been waiting with him for half an hour. Amir shook his head in disgust at his own explanation. For one thing he never explained things to his staff, or to anyone—to do so showed weakness—and for another, he should have gone to Ruby's room and dragged her down here as soon as she was one minute late.

Then he heard it. The regular metallic click of heel on stone getting ever louder. It reminded him of the metronome his piano teacher had used for his piano lessons. Turned out he had no musicality in his bones, but the rhythm and regularity of the metronome had stayed with him and he'd run his life along similar lines ever since—relentless, regular and controlled. Except now the control was coming from outside of him, from someone who threatened his world with each step she took. But someone with whom he was stuck because if she left, his world would collapse. He was, he thought, stuck between a rock and a hard place, as his English university friends would have said, and all he could do was battle each moment with Ruby.

The click of her footsteps came ever closer, and he turned away from the open doorway and fixed his gaze straight ahead to an ornately framed painting over the fireplace. He wondered what his great-grandfather would have made of the situation. No doubt he would have approved. The Al-Rahman family did whatever was required to look after family and fortune.

Then he inhaled her fragrance as she stood beside him. He glanced at her and wished he hadn't. She was striking, dressed in a blood red sheath, exactly the right shade of red to complement her coloring. Her violet eyes looked at him with a challenge in them. First battle of the day.

"You're late," he said.

"A bride's prerogative, surely."

He grunted. "Let's get on with it, shall we?"

"That's what I'm here for." She smiled sweetly.

He nodded for the celebrant to begin. He'd had his assistant select the briefest ceremony. As the celebrant spoke, his mind drifted to the woman beside him. She appeared to have no tension, no qualms about marrying him on this basis, and she held herself with supreme confidence. He'd never met anyone like her and she got to him, on so many levels, like no one else.

"Your Majesty?" The celebrant's question drew him back to the present. "You need to say 'I do.'"

He nodded. "I do."

"And do you, Ruby…"

He turned to watch Ruby, to see how she would cope with this charade. She'd used the same color lipstick as her dress. She opened her lips softly and then formed the words. He could scarcely drag his eyes from those lips, and he felt himself stir as he had no right to stir, as he remembered the magic and havoc they'd created on his body so many years ago.

Then she turned to him. "So, Amir, are you going to kiss the bride, like the man says?"

"Of course. It's traditional."

"I'm glad you said that," she murmured, as he closed in on her lips.

He'd meant to only press his lips briefly to hers but when his mouth met hers he remembered the taste of her and he decided that this might just be struggle number two, which he was going to win. He slipped his arm around her waist and felt her catch her breath with surprise, right before his mouth came over hers with a kiss which was designed to show her exactly who was in control of their relationship.

But somewhere between his intention and the act he forgot where he was. There was only the two of them and the faint whimper that came from her as he deepened the kiss. And when his tongue found hers, he held her closer, and for one exquisite moment she pressed her body to his. Then there was a loud bang and they drew apart. He looked around and there was confusion everywhere. Balloons, streamers filled the air, as did Hani's laughter as he batted a balloon, followed by streams of confetti that showered over them. Somehow, unnoticed by him, a fine net containing multi-colored heart-shaped confetti had been suspended over them, released when they'd kissed.

But before he could remonstrate, Hani had taken him by the hand. "Baba! Thank you. I have a lovely mama, now!" Instead of growling at them all, he found himself ruffling his boy's head. Hani's smiling face wiped anything else from his mind. Ruby's eyes caught his as they spilled out onto the terrace where, apparently, staff had set out a wedding breakfast without his knowledge. So much for him winning this battle. Every time he thought he was ahead, Ruby blindsided him. He wished he felt more angry about it. But how could he when his son was so obviously happy? Ruby had been here such a short amount of time, but she'd drastically altered the atmosphere in the palace, and changed his son from a nervous boy into a mischievous one. He was trying to figure out how he felt about that when Ruby came over to him with Hani.

"Give it to him, then," she said encouragingly to Hani.

Hani handed him a small gift wrapped up. "For me?" asked Amir, ludicrously touched by the gesture.

"Yes, Baba."

Hani looked hesitant and unsure. Amir opened the present, turned over the small flat thing in his hand and discovered a small picture of Hani and himself, delicately drawn and filled in with water color. He recognized the image. It must have been taken from the photo Ruby took of them when they'd gone for ice creams. He'd had famous artists paint family portraits—stiff images of Hani, Mia and himself. They were beautiful, valuable and excellent likenesses, then why was he so moved by this? He swallowed as he noted the way Hani had portrayed their physical closeness —shoulders bumped against each other, his arm around Hani, protecting him against the world.

"I made it myself. I wasn't sure if you'd like it but Ruby said you would."

"I do. Thank you." He should say more, he knew he should, but the truth was he daren't speak, his throat was constricted and he had no idea whether a sob or a word would emerge. He looked at Ruby, and she gave a brief nod, as if she understood. How could she understand when he didn't?

"Hani," said Ruby, "your friend is over there. See? The chef's son. Why don't you bring him over and get some food together? Remember what I said? Make him feel at home and included."

"Sure, Ruby."

The moment of emotion passed as Amir registered his son's response. Amir had never heard his son say 'sure' to anyone. It was such a western word and he was about to remonstrate with Ruby but she raised an eyebrow.

"Don't even start, Amir. This is our wedding day."

He closed his mouth and changed tack. "What did you think I was going to say? Rebuke you in some way? Maybe I was simply going to congratulate you on how well your relationship with Hani is growing. He seems very happy."

"He is. He doesn't appear in the least perturbed that I've only been here a short time and we're married."

He shrugged. "He's accustomed to that. Both my cousin's marriages were arranged."

"Arranged? What century do you live in? And I guess you were the one who arranged them?"

He shrugged again. This time a shade more uncomfortably. "I had some input into the decision, naturally."

"Naturally," she said, in a wry tone which wasn't lost on him. "So all this is normal in Hani's world."

"Yes. And, of course, he's not used to questioning anything. Whatever I decide, goes."

They turned to watch him playing with the other boy. "I guess in this case, it's worked, but I reckon he needs to question things if he's going to grow up to take control of his own life. You won't be here forever," she said, her lips tweaking in a perturbingly sexy way. "No matter what you believe."

"Maybe, but he needs to learn control and structure before he can make any kind of decision in his life. That is how it will be. I'll allow you both some fun, but there is no way you are going to change the direction I'm taking with Hani. Is that clear?"

"Crystal."

"Good."

"But—"

"No buts."

Those beautiful lips pressed together, but one errant eyebrow shot up and she turned away and stalked off, the tight-fitting red dress revealing the perfect curve of her butt. He quickly looked away, although it was his wife's butt, he reminded himself. It wasn't a hanging offense. But he was irritated. She hadn't responded but somehow that silence didn't satisfy him. Somehow, and he didn't know how, she'd walked away having won the argument. Yet again.

He watched her talk to staff as if they were guests. He suddenly realized that most of them appeared to be sipping the Moet and he sighed. She'd invited them. Of course she had. She might have accepted the fact that he'd refused to invite her model friends to the wedding—he'd be damned if he were going to have that hard-drinking bohemian crowd enter his palace—but she'd obviously decided to invite the staff instead. He never socialized with his staff. He avoided talking to them about anything other than work. Like it or not, Ruby was changing things. And he most definitely did *not* like it. He signaled for a glass of water. But the struggle for power wasn't over yet. He'd put her in her place the next day, only she didn't know it yet. Maybe then she'd learn.

RUBY SLIPPED OFF her shoes and tucked her feet under her on the leather couch in the formal room which she'd designated as a family room. She'd persuaded the staff to change the furniture around and make this room more inviting—a place where she and Hani could hang out. To her knowledge, Amir had never set foot inside this room and was still unaware of the change. She hoped it stayed that way, because this constant battle of wills was beginning to wear her out.

She'd given Hani's nanny the night off and had put Hani to bed herself. She'd sung him to sleep in the end, silly songs that she remembered from her own childhood, songs that no doubt went back generations, connecting some slender thread of family line, sending them all to sleep. She liked that thought. Family history was something she'd never had. Parents alienated from their families, a father dead before he was thirty and a sick mother had ensured she'd been able to stand on her own two feet from an early age. And here she was, with someone whose family went back to Machiavelli on his mother's side and no doubt Saladin on his father's side. With that pedigree, was it any wonder Amir drove her crazy?

She yawned and stretched out and turned on the TV. She didn't care what program was showing, because she also needed something to get her to sleep, the sound of people talking, the sound of activity, the sound of her not being alone.

AMIR LOOKED around in shocked surprise at what had once been his mother's drawing room. The drapes were the same, the wallpaper was the same, but practically everything else in it had changed. It no longer possessed a formal air and the trashy entertainment show which was showing on a new large screen TV was the vulgar icing on the ugly cake.

If he hadn't felt like things were getting out of control when all that confetti had filled the air—not to mention his eyes and mouth—then he did now. She'd gone too far. Then he saw her, curled up asleep, her blonde hair spread over the chic black cushion, like sunlight over a cloud. She tweaked something deep inside. It was the same whenever he was near her—she pulled a cord, plucked a string, made a connection, a vibration which resounded at its basest level inside him. He felt like a puppet, being manipulated by an expert puppet mistress. But now that expert puppet mistress was curled up fast asleep on a couch in front of the TV and she looked impossibly young—too young to be the mother of a five-year-old, and far too young to keep on out-maneuvering him quite so skilfully.

He stepped forward to awaken her but something stopped him and, instead, he allowed himself the pleasure of soaking up the sight before him. Her hair fell away from her face, her chin was uplifted onto the cushion, so she could see the TV better, and her lashes, darkened with makeup, were like Hani's—darker than their hair. It was warm in the room and her cheeks held a soft flush which helped with the impression of her youth. But there was nothing childish about her graceful arms folded across her slender body. She was beautiful, of that there was no doubt. But it was only now, when she lay fast asleep, that he realized the source of her beauty didn't lie in that slender body. When she was awake her presence and personality filled the room, entrancing everyone around her. Her spirit was even more beautiful than her body, and totally seductive.

He stepped away, picked up the remote and turned off the TV. He should leave but hesitated. She looked so vulnerable. He picked up another addition to the room—a pale pink mohair throw and gently, so as not to awaken her, laid it over her.

Her eyes opened wide immediately and she swung her legs off the couch and sat up. "Amir!"

He stepped away abruptly. "I'm sorry. I didn't mean to wake you."

She pushed her hands through her hair and cleared her throat, trying to throw off the shadows of sleep which still clung to her. "What are you doing?"

He dropped the blanket which he was still holding onto the couch and shrugged.

She looked down at the blanket and then back up at him. "Covering me with a blanket?" The last of the shadows evaporated and she smiled. "That's kind of you."

He grunted and shuffled, annoyed at having been caught in a weak moment. "Not kind. Simply…" He looked around, trying to find inspiration from anywhere, because he never started a sentence not knowing how it would end, unless he was in Ruby's orbit.

"Simply concerned that your new wife might get chilled. And you have to keep her fit and healthy, don't you?"

He sighed with relief. "Exactly. I'm glad you understand."

"I understand only too well." She walked over to the drinks cabinet and poured herself a brandy. She was still wearing the red dress which was now wrinkled and had hitched up around her body, revealing more of her lovely limbs. As he was admiring the view from behind, she took a sip before turning back to him. She folded one arm around her waist and swirled the drink in the other hand, inspecting him as he did her. "Care for a night cap?"

He shouldn't. He should leave, now, while he still could. "Yes." It wasn't the answer he'd meant to give.

She poured him a drink, and he suddenly felt as if he were a visitor in his own home. It should have irritated him, but it intrigued him more.

"Here." She held out the drink. She was forcing him to move closer to him. Yet another challenge.

He walked up to her, nearer than was necessary, and watched her blink with surprise as he took the drink from her. He'd moved into her personal space to show her she couldn't gain the upper hand on him, but he hadn't counted on the smell of her perfume, mellowed by the day, now mixed with the scent of her skin. He took a sip of the brandy to disguise his instinctive swallow. He swore to himself. He wanted to taste her neck, not the damn drink. "Thank you," he said instead.

She raised an eyebrow. "For what? The drink, or marrying you?"

"Both," he answered. He didn't know who was more surprised by his honest answer.

It was her turn to look confused. She bit her bottom lip in a way which did nothing to relieve his arousal and sat back on the couch. "I didn't think there was ever any doubt in your mind that I'd stay."

"Only stupid people have no doubt."

She looked up at him from beneath those long lashes which only moments before, he'd admired against her flushed cheek. Her cheeks were even more flushed now, he noticed. "And you're not stupid," she said.

"No." He found himself sitting opposite her. A coffee table squarely placed between them, a barrier to prevent him from reaching out, hooking his hand around her neck and pulling her face to his, her mouth to his, her lips to his. He took another sip of brandy. "I plan for doubt. One way or another you'd have stayed."

Disconcertingly she smiled, her violet eyes flashing with humor.

"What's so funny?"

She raised her eyebrows. "You. You're so macho."

"Machismo. It's simply a latin name for being masculine. You've been spending too much time with the wrong sort of people."

"By the wrong sort you mean people who actually listen to what I have to say, people who don't expect their every command to be obeyed, people who, God forbid, actually do as I say."

"You're wrong on one count. I do listen to what you have to say." He sat back and shrugged. "But if you talk nonsense then of course I ignore it."

"And it would be nonsense if you don't agree with it."

"Of course."

"Or maybe, if you don't allow yourself to agree with it."

"I don't need permission to believe something."

She placed her glass on the table and leaned forward. "I think you do. Would you like me to give you an example?"

He shifted in his seat, part of him wanting to escape

immediately from under Ruby's compelling blue gaze, and part of him enthralled by her and relishing the vibrations of attraction which hummed through his veins. "Go on. I suspect you're going to, with or without my agreement."

She rose and he was treated to a brief flash of her thighs before she pulled down the dress. She was barefoot and padded softly over the thick rug and perched on the table in front of him. "You see, you're attracted to me, I can see it in everything you do or don't do." She reached out and touched the corner of his eye, and he drew a sharp intake of breath. "In your eyes." She trailed a finger down his cheek and rested it on his lips. His groin tightened. "And there, definitely there, in your lips. When you see me, you lick them."

"I don't," he said, suddenly indignant at the image of him salivating before her like some adolescent.

"Oh yes, you do," she said softly. "But I don't mind. In fact"—she tipped her head to one side—"I quite like it. It does something to me." She placed her hand low on her stomach and he felt himself instantly hard. Her eyes flickered down as she took his drink from his hand and placed it on the table. "And then there's somewhere else where I affect you." She rose and he watched, spellbound, to see what she'd do. If she left now, he wasn't sure he'd be able to prevent himself from forcibly stopping her. But he didn't have to, because she poked out her wonderful butt and placed it on his lap. He groaned and let his head fall against the back of the chair as his erection was massaged by the soft flesh of her behind. "Yes." She leaned in to him, her bottom shifting slightly, finding its home over his rigid member. "I was right. You are attracted to me."

"Attracted?" He slipped his hands around her hips and drew her closer. "That is a weak word for what I feel."

"Then what word would suffice?" she asked, as if butter wouldn't melt in her mouth. But it would. He knew it would.

"None, I think. Maybe, in circumstances like this, words should be replaced by action."

It was his turn to see her lose control. He could feel her tremble as he pulled her to him. He had only one thought. To show her exactly who was in control of that moment.

Her lips tasted of brandy and lust. It was the last inadequate thought he had before his tongue swept along her lips and was met by hers. It was like the ignition of a spark to a tinder dry fire that had been parched for years, waiting for such a moment. Any thought of control was lost as their tongues tangled, their breathing quickened and their hands found each other like drowned people clasping to the other for dear life.

He swallowed her whimpers as his hands pushed up her dress to reveal her skimpy underwear. His hands caressed her bare bottom briefly before he hooked his thumbs around the g-string and pulled it down. She rose and let it fall to the floor. Her dress was still pushed up to her waist, leaving her sex naked and at eye level. He couldn't resist and pressed his lips to her sex and explored it hungrily, his tongue probing her until she trembled in his arms. He couldn't get enough of her. He wanted to taste her everywhere, feel inside her. As his fingers and mouth explored her body, her moans of pleasure turned to cries, and inside she pulsed around his fingers, soaking them in moisture, he drew her to him.

But instead of allowing him to continue to take control of her, she slid down his fly and pushed down his trousers and he found himself lying back on the couch, with her straddling him, easing herself onto him, while all he could do was lie back and watch her take pleasure from him. He thrust up into her and was rewarded by a flickering of her eyelids and a mouth open and inviting. But then he waited. He wanted her on edge, he wanted her to want him as much as he wanted her.

Her eyes opened, a slight frown on her face as she moved on him but he stayed put. Then he thrust deeply into her and she gasped with surprise at the abrupt sensation. He did this once more and then she did something which took him by surprise. She looked at him from behind lowered lids and with one movement, swept her dress over her head, unclipped her bra and threw it to one side. She shook her hair and leaned forward, her breasts grazing his chest, riding him, squeezing him with a regularity which had him roaring as he lifted her and lay her on the floor, holding out her spread hands in a fierce grip. But it was the only part of her that was under control. Her legs were wrapped around his hips, as he thrust repeatedly into her, unable to stop now even if the palace was on fire and the place was inundated with people. She had him in his thrall, and he had only one focus, to come into her, to spill his seed deep inside her and make her his own.

With one last thrust he came into her, more and more, filling her with himself, still pumping into her with small movements as if he'd never fill her.

She was right. She brought out the primitive animal in him. He'd read somewhere that if men suspected their woman of sleeping with another man, their sperm was more plentiful, as if making sure they would dominate. He knew this was what had happened. He was making her his as surely as if he were shackling to her to him with a ball and chain. Had he gone mad?

He pulled out and looked down at her as her hand trailed down to where he recently been, spreading the wet trail of his sperm onto her clitoris. She trembled slightly. And he stepped back once more. She was like a drug to him. He doubted he'd ever get enough. But she brought out something that scared the hell out of him.

She must have sensed it because she rose and stood naked before him. "What is it?"

He shook his head. "I have to go."

She snaked her hand behind his neck and brought him close to her and kissed him thoroughly, until his erection was hard again. She pulled away and glanced down. "Really?"

"Yes, really."

She bit her lip and the sudden insecurity in her eyes pricked at his undefended heart. Damn!

She turned away and pulled on her dress in silence and, by the time she turned around he was also dressed.

"Are you coming to bed?" she asked, in a vulnerable whisper which by-passed any remaining defenses and shot to the heart of him.

He shook his head, not trusting himself to speak, for fear of what would emerge, what words of need he'd speak out loud. He couldn't hand himself to her on a plate, to do with as she liked. He'd done that once with devastating results.

"Okay." She gave a brief smile which twisted the knife in his heart.

She closed the door behind him and he tossed back his brandy. As the fiery liquor raced through his body, he made a decision.

It was clear that she was his Achilles' Heel and it was also clear that he couldn't trust himself around her. He wanted to lose himself in her, gain respite in her from the world he'd created in which he was alone, but he couldn't. To do anything like that would be to lose all that he'd gained, to jeopardize all that he had. No, there was only one solution.

He walked along the empty ancient corridors to his office and contacted his overseas offices to make the necessary arrangements. Once done, he poured himself another brandy. He looked into its amber depth. Another thing he rarely did, drink alcohol. Not like this. It seemed he was losing control in every aspect of his life. It couldn't go on. He needed space.

He replaced the glass and switched out the light. She'd hate him, he realized. But wouldn't that be easier to live with than lust?

CHAPTER 6

*J*t was late morning by the time Ruby awoke. She'd slept well for a change and, as she stretched out over the fine silk sheets, her mind dwelled on the reason for the feeling of well-being which lingered in her relaxed limbs. She inhaled a long breath as she closed her eyes and replayed Amir's love-making in her mind.

It had been literally mind-blowing and, with her mind having been well and truly blown, her body had taken over, as had his. The sex had held echoes of their love-making five years earlier, but what had happened last night had been just that—sex. There'd been no sense of the love they'd used to feel for each other, only a desperate need to sate their lust.

She sighed and rolled her head to look out the window. It was light. The sun was already high and there was no sea breeze to alleviate the heat which rolled in from the desert and settled over the palace and city below it. She glanced at the clock and wondered why she hadn't been called, as she'd requested. She'd wanted to rise earlier so as to spend time with Hani at breakfast, before his school day began, but no one had rung her and her body clock stubbornly adhered to her old lifestyle.

Where was everyone? She pulled on a robe and squinted out at the bright light. Usually there was some kind of activity outside the window, at the very least gardeners tending the lush blooms which wouldn't last a day without their care under the intense heat of the sun. But this morning there was no one, no sign of any activity.

Frowning, she went to the bathroom, turned on the shower and rang Amir. It went straight to voicemail which wasn't unusual. But, she considered as she ended the call without leaving a message, what *was* unusual was the message. It was a new recorded message, not from Amir, but from his assistant. He'd obviously had Ruby's calls transferred directly to his assistant. That, she decided, as she slipped off her robe and stepped into the fierce shower, was not a good sign. Did he regret what happened last night? But how could he, when it was what he wanted? Even if he hadn't wanted her, which she knew he did, he'd wanted a brother or sister for Hani. That had been part of the agreement after all.

But as her mind re-ran the events of the previous night, she understood. She'd initiated it, he'd lost control and he was scared. He never lost control. And if he couldn't help himself when he was close to her, then he'd put distance between them. As she moved her body under the flow of water, washing the traces of their lovemaking away, she had to admit there was logic to his actions. But what she needed to know was exactly how far he proposed to remove her from him, and from Hani.

But half an hour later, when she was walking through the eerily quiet private wing of the palace, she was no further in understanding what had happened. The place seemed deserted. She'd been to both Amir's and Hani's bedrooms. Both were tidy and aired as if no one had spent the night there. She'd lingered a few moments in Hani's room, lifting his pillow to inhale his little boy's scent. She trailed her fingers across his small book case filled with old and modern classics in classy bindings, many of which were too difficult for him to read, and briefly looking inside his dressing room, smiling at the small suits which looked incongruous to her. But she didn't stay long, because it wasn't his things she wanted to see, but him.

The story was the same downstairs. For such a large palace, there didn't seem to be anyone around. No one in the drawing room or family rooms. She stopped at the library door and knocked, and when there was no reply, she entered. It was empty, just like the other rooms. But here, like in Hani's room, she couldn't help lingering.

The smell of books engulfed her and she closed her eyes as memories swept into her mind—of her childhood home, the small sitting room, packed floor to ceiling with books. She'd used to be embarrassed to bring her friends home because their mothers would be in a tidy kitchen, cooking dinner. At first it hadn't been so bad—her mother would have been reading, ignoring life as if she were an island, buoyed by books, around which the tide of life could sweep, but not touch her. But, later, as her illness had progressed, she'd retreated beyond even where her books could touch her. She'd simply sit, staring out at the dead-end road, along which no traffic came, no visitors. On days like that, Ruby just got on and focused on things like food for them both. She dealt with the practical things and tried to put out of her mind the fact that her mother hardly moved from the room. The smell of books brought it all back.

Ruby retreated from the room, as equal measures of panic and sadness settled in her heart. She walked quickly away, pushing the memories to the back of her mind, looking around for distraction but finding none. She flung open the french windows, needing the hot air to sweep away the sticky memories which clung to her mind, threatening to stifle the life out of it. She strode out onto the front terrace that looked out over the old city and harbor and gulped down the air, a little cooler here, but felt no comfort.

She turned around and retreated indoors, found the music system and flicked it on. Sound filled the air and her head but it didn't drown out her thoughts. She left the room and went toward the kitchen and offices. Surely there would be someone there. The emptiness was beginning to panic her. She practically ran into the stone-flagged family kitchen, whose walls and beamed ceiling were some of only a few original features in the kind of state-of-the-art kitchen required by the imperial family of Janub Havilah. The panic ebbed a little when she found two kitchen staff busy preparing food.

"Hello! Thank goodness I've found someone. Can you tell me where the king and Hani are?"

The staff looked from one to the other. "They are not here, madam."

"Right," she said, trying to rein in her irritation. Yesterday she'd chatted with these people easily, but today was obviously another day and something had happened to make them avert their gaze nervously, and revert to their old form of address. "Could you please tell me, where are they?" She folded her arms across her waist and gave them the stare which had put hundreds of photographers and directors in their places. Kitchen staff, apparently, were of a hardier breed.

"They're gone, madam."

Ruby sighed. This wasn't going to be over quickly. "And might you tell me where they've gone?"

The man who'd spoken shrugged and turned back to cleaning the silver. Incensed, she walked up to him, and was about to question him further when both men looked nervously at the door, where Amir's assistant, Jamal, had suddenly appeared.

"Ah, Jamal, just the man I need to see."

"Good morning, madam." Jamal stood aside and indicated the passageway to Ruby. "Would you care to come to my office?"

She had to stifle her immediate reply. While Jamal's words were to be expected from a staff member, his attitude, expressed in the sly way he looked at her, showed quite the opposite. "Sure," she said shortly, and stalked out of the kitchen.

She knew where his office was and didn't wait for him to open it, but flung it open and took a seat before he could take the upper hand and offer her one.

"Now, Jamal, perhaps you'll tell me what the hell is going on?"

Jamal walked around the other side of his desk, upon which a slim computer sat, with a near constant stream of emails being delivered. His kingdom was obviously ruled with as much severity and control as the mirror one of Amir's, above stairs.

He steepled his fingers. "In what way, madam?"

"Do I have to spell it out?"

"Yes, I think you do."

This man would have to go. One way or another she'd make sure of it. In the meantime she had to play him at his own game.

She forced a studied smile on her face. "Jamal, have you seen Amir and Hani this morning?"

"Of course, madam." Jamal looked at her with a dignified blankness which seemed to be characteristic of the palace officials. It only ignited irritation in Ruby. She raised an eyebrow.

87

"Can you tell me where they are?"

"I'm sorry, madam, I cannot."

She leaned forward. "Cannot or will not?"

Jamal nodded his head with a smile. "Both. The effect is the same."

Ruby's anger spiked but she pushed it down. It wouldn't get her anywhere here. "I see. Perhaps if I keep my questions focused, your answers will be equally so. Deal?"

Jamal bowed his head in polite agreement. She sucked in a deep, controlling breath. "Has Hani's condition worsened?" It was the fear which underlay everything.

His smile didn't falter. "No, not to my knowledge."

She stood up. "Then tell me where he is."

"He is fine. He's with His Majesty, King Amir."

"That is not telling me where he is!"

Jamal looked at his watch with studied slowness. "By this time? I believe they'll be landing in Boston."

She sat down as if she'd been pushed. "The US?"

"Yes." He plucked a piece of paper from a pile.

"How long will they be there?"

"Hani will be there a week, I believe."

"Hani, but not Amir?"

Jamal shrugged.

"Then I wish you to organize tickets so I can be with Hani."

"Apologies, madam, but I have strict instructions that you are not to follow. Everything is in hand, everything under control, and Hani will be home by the end of the week."

"I wish to go."

"And His Majesty *doesn't* wish for you to go." Jamal licked his lips as if about to digest something delicious. "He doesn't wish Hani to be disturbed by the presence of a stranger."

An electric charge shot through her. "A stranger? Do you know who I am, Jamal?"

His face didn't flicker, didn't betray any kind of emotion or knowledge. "Of course. You are married to His Royal Highness, the king of Janub Havilah."

She raised her eyebrows in query, knowing full well that he must be aware of the situation. "And as queen, I wish to be with my son."

He shook his head. "His Majesty has left precise instructions." He reached out for a piece of paper and slid it across the desk to her. "This is for you. I took the liberty of printing out your schedule for the forthcoming week. His Majesty wishes you to focus on getting yourself in top physical condition." The man's insulting gaze briefly swept her body. She'd never felt more like a piece of meat, not even when photographed, never felt so humiliated.

She stood up and took the piece of paper from him and tore it in half and tossed it back to him. "Thank you, Jamal, but that won't be necessary."

She turned and left the room, reaching for her phone as she went. She continued walking outside to the terrace and beyond. She didn't stop until she came to the ornamental garden, beyond the sight or sound of people observing her. This time she did leave a message—it was short and to the point. His face appeared moments later on her phone screen.

"How dare you blackmail me!" he said.

"If threatening to tell the papers all about you and me and anything else I can think of, or invent, is the only way to get you to ring me then that's what I'll do! I want to know why you've suddenly taken Hani away." Her voice faltered on his name. She couldn't help it. Overwhelming her anger was her fear for her son. "Tell me, is he okay?"

Amir sighed. "Yes. He's okay."

It was the relief which made her anger flare. "Then where the hell is he?"

"As I asked Jamal to inform you, we are in the US. Boston to be exact."

"Amir! I don't understand. Yesterday—"

"Yesterday we had some fun and today it's business again."

"Hani *is* my business."

"Why do you say that?"

"Oh, I don't know, maybe because I'm his natural mother."

He looked around to make sure no one was listening. "Do not talk of yourself as his natural mother in public."

She refused to be cowed. He might control everyone else, but she'd never allow him to control her. "Why not? It's the truth."

"Perhaps. But it is not a palatable one."

"It is to me."

"But this isn't about you. It's about Hani. And he needs what you can do for him right now."

"He needs my blood, but not me as a mother, I suppose you mean."

"I'm glad you understand so well."

Ruby grunted with frustration. "Amir, why have you taken him away? Just tell me that."

He didn't answer.

"For the love of God, tell me."

"I'd prefer not to at the moment."

"Why?"

"I have my reasons."

"You can't do this to me! You can't let me get close only to take him away again. It's cruel."

He shrugged. "Maybe I am."

And she knew in that instant, in the expression in his eyes, that he didn't want to believe it of himself. And she knew damn well that she didn't believe it. "No you're not.

You never used to be. And I don't think you are now. For some reason, you don't want to tell me. I wonder why."

He licked his lips and his eyes flickered over her face. He looked around and the background changed as he walked into a different room.

"There's a consultant here in Boston who we've been working with. She's been analyzing the results from Hani's treatment and asked to see him."

"And you didn't tell me?"

"No. You need to be there to get yourself ready for the hospital. If this doesn't work, the consultant says that the…" He hesitated and frowned. "The *procedure* will be needed as soon as possible. Now I have to go. While Hani and I are away you will be subject to a strict regime of fitness, diet and medical supervision in readiness."

There was a silence and his gaze drifted from hers. "Why did you say 'procedure' like that?"

"Like what?" he replied shortly, the frown deepening.

"Like it's more than a simple procedure."

He didn't respond. Someone called from behind him. "I have to go."

His answer, or lack of it, told her more than she wanted to know.

She swayed a little and sat down on a nearby seat. He was keeping something from her, something she wouldn't like, because it would be bad for her, or for Hani. She suspected both.

"Are you all right?" he asked.

She looked back at the phone. For once there was a look of concern on Amir's face which almost robbed her of her anger, almost make her weak and vulnerable but only 'almost'. She nodded.

"You *will* still do this for Hani?" Amir asked.

Fear nibbled at her body and her heart and soul. Behind

Amir's fierce gaze she could see a terror which equalled her own and she knew its source. He was terrified she'd let him down, which could spell the end of Hani's life. How had it ever happened that Amir could believe such a thing of her?

"Of course I will. I've told you I'll do anything for him."

"Good. Then begin on the regime which Jamal has given you. We'll be back by the end of the week."

She nodded and switched off the phone first. She looked around her, stunned. The world still looked the same, but everything had changed. She was being forced to face a terror from which she'd been running the past five years. It seemed her time was up. She'd have to face hospital—and some kind of procedure which Amir was too scared to tell her about—and her worst fears.

RUBY SOMEHOW MANAGED to evade an actual hospital visit over the week when Hani and Amir were away. But she ate what was put in front of her and used Amir's gym to increase her fitness. But still the domestic wing of the palace was empty and the lack of people and activity was oppressing her more each day.

This was what her life was going to be like. On her own. Like her mother. And, like her mother, she'd be prey to the darkness of spirit that seeped into your soul stealthily at first. Then, when you finally noticed its presence, it was too late. It engulfed you.

She snatched a lungful of air, as if she were suffocating. She wasn't her mother. She *wasn't* her mother, she repeated with more force. She had choices. She had people she could turn to. But here, away from her usual support network, she felt isolated and alone in a way she hadn't been in years.

The evenings were the worst. Like now, she thought, as

she walked along the empty corridors. Amir had said that the palace was to be her home, but she wondered if he knew the meaning of the word. A more "un-homelike" place she'd yet to see. Every wall bore a proud portrait of one of his ancestors, and every sideboard either featured photographs of Amir's dead wife, or priceless china from centuries ago, which Hani was never allowed to go near. It was like a morgue, a gallery, a museum dedicated to people and institutions long dead.

It needed life, she thought, as she straightened a painting of a woman, beautifully dressed and seated serenely amidst half a dozen children "I bet you didn't have to worry about a thing, did you?" She tilted her head to one side as she inspected the family group. If this family had lived here—and it looked like they had, from the background of port and sea, which had barely been touched in hundreds of years—these corridors wouldn't have been as quiet as they were now. No, the place demanded a family. Ruby narrowed her eyes as she looked around at the beautiful spaces. No, she thought again, it demanded people. And didn't she know where she could get those?

She glanced at her watch. It was late. She'd done what she'd promised Amir, up till now. She hadn't contacted the photographer who'd was shooting a designer collection at the port. But she knew they were still there. It would have been hard to ignore them as they featured heavily in the social media of all her friends. They were in the country for just two more days. And, while it was late, her friends partied late. As she rang the photographer she pondered on whether she was breaking Amir's protocol. But in all the memories of him telling her what she could and couldn't do, none of it concerned the possibility of her inviting people over. No doubt the possibility hadn't even entered his head.

She sat back with a grin as the ringtone was answered.

"Angelo? It's Ruby." She listened to a drunken shout of greeting followed by a barrage of questions. "I'll tell you when I see you. What are you doing tonight?"

THE PALACE WAS NOW EXACTLY as she liked it. Angelo had arrived with a dozen or so of her friends and acquaintances, who were either dancing, chatting or drinking, or all three. It may have been only a dozen, but they made the noise of two dozen. For the first time in weeks, the panic which always nudged to the front of Ruby's mind was quieted, soothed by the noise and activity. Since the crippling post-natal depression she'd suffered after giving birth to Hani, this had been her only solace—a hum of activity and noise which de-stressed her like nothing else. Over the years people had mistaken it for many things, but she hadn't revealed the cause to anyone. The memory of her mother's illness was much too vivid. No, the only way to keep a secret was to tell no one. That much she'd learned from life. And so, her friends carried on around her while she sat back on the couch, sipping soda water, letting their shouts of laughter and antics bathe her wounds.

The music was loud but Ruby wasn't concerned. The staff vacated the family wing at night and they were quite alone. There was no one they could disturb and it felt good not to be afraid, for once, of being watched or overheard. She was among friends now.

She pushed off her shoes and tucked them under her and sat back on the soft cushions. Angelo grabbed one of her feet and started to massage it. Ruby closed her eyes—her mind and body soothed by the noise. Slowly it receded, leaving only a hum. She sighed and within moments was asleep, making up for the countless hours she'd lain awake since she'd arrived in the palace.

. . .

RUBY AWOKE WITH A START. She was seated by herself now. It took a moment for her to remember where she was, so deep had been her sleep. Then she rubbed her eyes and looked around, trying to figure out what had awoken her. The music was even louder than before—she didn't know how she'd been able to sleep through it, and didn't know what could have been even louder to disturb her. She got to her feet and looked around.

She picked up a couple of empty wine bottles, still dusty from the cellar. Her friends hadn't wasted any timing in tracking down Amir's wine. She blanched when she looked at its label. She wasn't a drinker but even she knew that this was priceless stuff.

"Hey!" She called out to no one in particular. There were more people here now than when she'd fallen asleep. She searched their faces in the dim light. And, she suddenly realized, she barely knew half of them. Word had obviously got about and the numbers had swollen to at least three times as many. There must have been over fifty people either dancing to the pounding beat or moving in the shadows, doing goodness knows what. Any sense of peace was instantly shattered by the realization that the party had gotten out of control. There was a crash and she winced at what might had shattered onto the stone floor.

She grabbed the first person she bumped into. "The party's over." But her voice was lost amid the din. "The party's over!" she yelled, louder now. But no one moved, the music continued, making her head ring. She grabbed at the next person who, with relief, she realized she knew. "Angelo!" She had to get closer and shout in his ear. "The party's over. All these people have to go!"

He grinned and leaned into her, his arm still firmly

around the waist of a woman she'd never seen before. "What's that, *cara*?"

"They've got to go!"

"But they've only just arrived."

"Who are they? I don't know half of them."

"Friends of mine. This place is wonderful, and as you were fast asleep I thought I'd invite a few more people round."

"A few more? Christ, Angelo, this must be half the population of Janub Havilah here, not to mention stray tourists."

"Not even half. I can bring the rest in, if you like."

"No way! They have to leave. Now!"

"But they've only just arrived. Party, *cara*. You do remember how to party, don't you? It's what you like to do. Come here." He let go of the woman and wrapped his arms around Ruby. "And let me show you."

He slammed her against his body and she was almost winded by the impact. Before she could recover, he'd wrapped his arms around her in a vice-like grip from which she couldn't move, and he'd dipped his head to hers and kissed her full on the lips. She brought her hands flat against his chest and tried to push him away, but he increased his hold and deepened the kiss. He tasted of wine, smoke and lipstick from the other women he'd kissed that night. Disgusted, she managed to push him away enough to break the kiss. But, for a slender-built man, he was strong and he held on tight. Indignation filled her and she wriggled, trying to get away from him, but he only tightened his grip.

"Angelo! What the hell—"

But her words were lost as he pressed his drunken lips to hers once more.

WHAT ON EARTH *was that noise?* Amir turned off the Ferrari's engine and heard the deep, bass throbbing of party music. It was three in the morning. What the hell was going on? He jumped out of the car and leaped up the wide steps to the palace's private quarters. It should have been locked but the double-doors were wide open, leaving the priceless antiques, paintings, and sculptures open wide to anyone who cared to take them. And, from the look of a couple of people running awkwardly across the lawn toward a car, it appeared they *were* being taken. He stopped, made a call on his phone, barked out a few orders, before finishing the call and continuing inside. He'd given Jamal leave of absence for a few days but he'd make sure that no one would escape the palace's grounds this night.

A couple were kissing in the hallway but all he did was push past them with a growl and move on toward the source of the sound. He had to push past more people, some actually making love in the shadows, fueled by unknown drugs, but still he ignored them, driven on by a fear about what else he'd see. The music came to him in throbs and waves down the long corridor to the reception room. Everything around him seemed to slow as he pushed forward on into the room, where he was met with a blast of alcohol and music. He stopped then and turned on the light. People cried out but he ignored them as his eyes zeroed in on Ruby. Even amongst so many people in different states of undress, dancing, drinking and moving to the music, he saw her, her body pressed up to another man, her lips pressed hard to another man's.

Anger, fierce and white-hot, filled his veins. Even as he moved towards them, pushing people aside, he could see she was struggling to get away. It made him more mad. He was beside them in a moment and grabbed the man by the scruff of his shirt neck. Yanking him off Ruby, he tossed him away as if he were weightless.

Without taking his eyes off Ruby, he shouted to his people who'd appeared following his summons.

"Get them out of here! Now!" His voice cut through the sound of the music and laughter and chatter of the people. It was aimed at his people, but his eyes hadn't moved from Ruby's.

RUBY RUBBED her hand across her mouth, wanting the taste of Angelo gone. Wanting them all gone. She'd got what she wanted, they'd come, bringing with them the noise and vibrancy of their world. But something had changed and they'd brought something unwanted into this world. Tears of shame pricked her eyes as she watched Amir, watching her, as his men swiftly ejected everyone from the premises. It didn't take long because Amir's men turned out to be not so polite as her guests were used to. Within moments the room was clear and Amir and Ruby were alone, surrounded by the detritus of a party.

"What the hell, Ruby?" She'd never seen Amir so angry. He was almost shaking. She shook her head and turned away. He grabbed her arm. "Don't turn away from me! I want to know what you were thinking, bringing this... this *rabble*, into my home. Into *Hani's* home, for Christ's sake."

"I can explain."

"Go on then, I'm waiting."

"Let me go, first." She tried to wriggle her wrist from his grip. "You're hurting me."

"Not until you tell me what the hell was going on here."

He jerked her arm and the action sent her wild with anger. "What do you think was going on, hey, Amir? It was a party! And no small wonder you don't recognize a party when you see one!"

"I know what a party is. What I've never associated with a

party is people stealing from my home, or strangers making love in the hall, helping themselves to my wine cellar. What the hell were you thinking of?" He shook her arm. "No need to tell me. I know exactly what you were thinking of. Yourself! As always."

She hadn't realized the friends of her friends had taken such liberties. "I'm sorry, I didn't know."

"Didn't know? What kind of defense is that? I saw you. With that man!" He tossed her arm away as if she were worthless to him, which she was, of course. She only had value in relation to the fact that she was his son's mother.

"I'm sorry, Amir, but I was alone. I hate being alone. You have no idea…"

"And is that what you're going to do? Whenever things don't go quite your way, bring your so-called friends into my home and trash it?"

He gripped her arm and she grimaced. "It wasn't like that."

"That's certainly what it looks like."

"I'm going to bed." She tried to pull away but his hand was firm on hers. "Amir? I…" But her voice trailed away as she saw the look in his eyes. Instead of letting her go, he dragged her closer to him. His face was so close to hers she could smell a trace of whiskey on his breath, could see the stubble on his chin. He'd obviously been in a hurry to return to Janub Havilah.

"No. Not this time. This time you don't run from me."

His eyes were dark and angry. He grabbed her by the other arm and pulled her until she was tight against him, until his mouth was close to hers while he spoke.

She lifted her chin to face him defiantly. "I haven't done anything wrong. You invited me to stay here, remember."

"I asked you to stay here for our son's sake. And what have you done?" His breath was hot on her face as he dipped his mouth closer to hers. His eyes roamed her face, taking in small parts, one eye then another, as if searching for some kind of answer. "You've turned it into a tawdry party scene just like the one you left behind." His fingers bit into her skin and she gasped. But her gasp drew his mouth to hers and he pressed his lips against hers with the same urgency his hands continued to hold her arms. She couldn't move. At first she kept her lips closed. It was the only defense against the assault. But he enclosed both her hands in one of his and, with the other, pulled her against his body. She felt him then and suddenly was aware of how aroused he was.

She felt his tongue and opened her mouth to caress it with her own. Their breathing came heavy as their minds and bodies became focused on their tongues that tangled with a raw sexuality that shifted down their bodies until they were tight against each other, moving against each other.

He suddenly let go of her hands and shifted both his hands under her bottom and lifted her against him. She slid her legs around him, the tight, stretchy dress sliding up until his hands found the bare flesh which her G-string didn't cover. He groaned and slid a finger round and found where she was wet. She gasped against his mouth and lifted her head. His mouth found her neck then, as he continued to slide his finger inside her. Then two fingers. She gulped and buried her face in his hair as she tried to regain some sense of control. But there was none. She moved against his hand, against the hardness of him, and came suddenly. She gasped again and again against his hair, her eyes blind to all that was around, as white light splintered through her.

He didn't wait until she'd finished but pulled her down roughly. Then he grabbed her hand and pulled her out of the room.

CHAPTER 7

*S*he had to run to keep up with him. She would have stumbled on the stairs if it weren't for his support, lifting her as she fell, propelling them forward with a need she could sense in his every movement. He slammed through his bedroom doors, kicked them shut and swung her round until she fell on the bed. He shrugged off his jacket, kicked off his shoes, yanked open his tie and shirt, and undid his trousers and stepped out of them.

She wriggled back, suddenly a little afraid of the sheer, determined look in his eyes. But that fear was overwhelmed by her need for him. She'd never felt more turned on by anyone since... Amir, she realized. He didn't say a word, simply caught her feet and pulled her along the bed to him. He tore off her g-string and, as she wrapped her legs around him, he entered her with one deep thrust. He closed his eyes as if he'd been struck and stayed completely still for a moment. Then he must have registered the sensation of her hands moving over his back and around his bottom, holding him where he was, because he opened his eyes, held her gaze, pulled out and thrust back into her again. He pulled out again and pushed again. Slapping into her with his body, melting away every other feeling than the blatant fact that he was claiming her.

He didn't kiss her, just held himself above her, dominating her with his will, his body, piercing her with himself, thrusting himself to her very core until she ceased to exist. She cried out as her orgasm swept her away but he didn't stop. His concentration was absolute. He continued thrusting and withdrawing, slowly increasing the pace until she came once more and only then did he come, pulsing inside of her, losing himself in her.

She watched as his eyes gradually lightened, became focused once more, and blinked with some expression she'd have named pain in any other circumstance. He pulled out and stepped away.

"I'm sorry," he said, shaking his head, his brows knit in confusion. "I'm so sorry."

She rolled to her side and dragged the covers over her nakedness. "There's no need to be sorry. You didn't do anything we both weren't wanting."

He looked at her then, a puzzled frown. "You wanted this? Like this?"

She shook her head, trying to think straight. "Wanted? My mind, if I'd been able to think about it, might have wanted something different. But my body"—she shrugged—"wanted exactly what you gave me."

"It should never have happened. Not like this."

She swallowed, her mouth suddenly dry. She sat up, shivered and pulled the cover around her shoulders. "A little foreplay might have been nice, but…" She looked up to see if her small attempt at humor had worked. It hadn't. He was dressing as if to leave. "But don't you understand, Amir? It was you I wanted. You."

"That wasn't me. That was someone out of control." He

shook his head again. "It wasn't me." He strode over to the door.

"Where are you going, Amir? This is your room."

He pushed his fingers through his hair, again not facing her. "I have to leave."

"Where are you going?"

"Anywhere. Don't you see, Ruby? You drive me crazy. I'm not myself when I'm with you. And I need to be. I *have* to be."

He left, closing the door quietly. She listened to his footsteps move quickly down the stone-flagged hall and away. She listened as his car roared into life and he sped off to God only knew where.

She collected her things and, wrapped only in a bed cover, went to her room and turned on the shower. He might have regretted it, but she couldn't, because she knew now how strong their need was for each other. They'd both repressed it for too long and their fierce coupling had been inevitable. The pendulum had swung hard in the other direction. But it would settle. It *had* to settle.

RUBY LAY AWAKE the remainder of the night listening to the deep silence. After the craziness of the evening, the silence seemed more glaring, more obtrusive than ever, crowding in on her and her thoughts. She'd never felt more alone, nor more angry with herself. How could she have let the night get out of hand, as it had?

At six she heard the staff come in and begin to clean up. She blushed, imagining what they were thinking and saying to each other. For the most past she'd established good relationships with them. What would they think of her now? Amir wouldn't worry about such things, but she liked people, she didn't want them to think badly of her. And they would. How could they not, when she thought badly of herself?

And then there was the sex. She couldn't call it love-making because it had nothing to do with love—it was all about possession. But it wasn't a one-way thing. No, she wanted to be possessed by him sexually, as much as he wanted to possess her. Intellectually, it worried her—it felt twisted, wrong. But another part of her dismissed her concerns, because it had also felt so right. And she knew that, if it were twisted, it was only because of the tensions and pressures they were both living under. Given the right circumstances, it could be as pure as it had once been.

And then there was Hani... In Boston, surrounded by loving staff, but not his family. Of all the mess, it was Hani who was uppermost in her mind—the rest she could handle. But Hani? Whether he or Amir knew it, Hani needed *her*, not paid staff, to look after him. And that was what she'd focus on. If he wasn't coming home anytime soon, then she'd just have to go to him.

She sat at her laptop, made some plans, and waited until she heard Amir arrive home. She heard him walk past her room and enter his own and the shower in the next bathroom switch on. She was in a hurry to tell him her plans, but if there was one thing she knew about men, it was better to talk to them after breakfast, and he always breakfasted with his advisors. After that he'd return to the solitude of his office for an hour before returning to fulfill his official duties for the rest of the day. She'd time her meeting for his hour of solitude.

An hour later, her bag packed and wearing a white white-legged pant suit and sharply cut jacket, she went downstairs to his office. She knocked on the door. There was a grunt she took to be agreement and she entered.

He looked up and frowned. "I'm busy."

She smiled sweetly. "As am I."

"Then I suggest you leave."

"No." She walked up to his desk and sat carefully on the chair in front, and crossed her legs. "My business is with you."

He grunted again, and looked back at his paperwork. He didn't say anything as he signed a paper, moved it to another pile and picked up another document, sitting back in his chair to read it. The clock ticked but he made no effort to respond to her.

She sighed. The man was impossible. "You can listen or not, that is up to you. But I will tell you what I've come here to say."

He turned over a page of the document he was reading, his frown deepening in concentration.

"Just for you," she continued, "I'll give it to you in bullet points. Firstly, I'm sorry about last night. The party," she added, because she wasn't sorry about what had happened later, even if he was. "It was stupid of me."

It seemed groveling caught his attention. He looked up, his expression blank. "Yes, it was."

"It won't happen again."

"No, it won't." He looked back at his papers, and brought up a pen and initialed a page.

She sucked her teeth in irritation. She'd expected the usual argument, at least some ranting, instead he was agreeing with her.

"You sound pretty sure that it won't," she said.

"Indeed."

She re-crossed her legs and jiggled her foot. "You're a man of few words this morning."

She was granted another look, less blank, slightly darker than before, before he resumed signing the paperwork before him on the desk.

"Okay, have it your way. Secondly, Hani."

He pushed his paperwork away and gave her his full attention. "What about him?"

"He shouldn't be in Boston alone."

"He's not alone. His nanny is with him, as well as three other staff who he knows well."

"They are not family. I am. I've made arrangements to travel to the US this evening to be with him."

"That is not necessary."

She jumped up and leaned over him, gripping the edge of the desk. "It is! How can you sit there so calmly and tell me Hani doesn't need his parents with him?"

"I'm not."

"You're not what?" If he was trying to confuse her, he was succeeding.

"Hani *does* need us, that is why my jet is being prepared as we speak, to return to Boston."

"You were going to return without telling me?" Cold fury filled her veins.

"No. I'd instructed Jamal to inform you." He glanced at his watch. "We'll be leaving this evening."

"I'm going too! There's no way you're going to leave me behind—"

"I said 'we'—"

"And how you could do such a thing is beyond me—"

"I said 'we'—" he repeated.

"I am his mother for goodness sake! His mother! How could you forget that!"

"Believe me, I cannot."

She suddenly replayed his words in her head. They were the opposite of what she was expecting. "You said 'we'. You mean you and Jamal, right?"

"Yes. And you."

"Oh!" She exhaled and walked away, trying to sort it in her head. "So you're not angry with me about last night?"

"It would be like being angry with a child."

She ground her teeth. "I am *not* a child, as you well know!"

"Ah, yes, maybe not in the bedroom, but you are in possession of a child's need for entertainment, for constant activity."

"You don't understand."

He rose, angry now. At last she'd broken through that reserve. "What I understand is that I need to control anything which threatens to disrupt my family or my kingdom. You're right, there will be no repeat of last night because I'm going to make sure you don't leave my sight. I'm going to make sure that your need for company is met, and that you aren't tempted into any more displays of idiocy like last night. I will control you, Ruby, so you'd better get used to it. Because I will not have my family destroyed by your chaos." He picked up a phone. "Here, take this. Jamal has loaded it with everything you need to know about the forthcoming trip."

She'd got a response all right, but it wasn't the one she'd expected. He'd turned the power struggle right around again. She shook her head. "You're impossible, Amir!"

"I'm sure that is true."

"And I hate you!"

He shook his head. "And there you are wrong." He walked up to her and she held her breath, as his eyes roved over her face before coming to rest on her lips. He licked his own lips and she felt an echo of his need deep inside her, in a part of her which felt well used from the previous night. Well used, but still ready for this man who dominated her mind and body. He handed her the phone. Her fingers briefly brushed his as they curled around it. It took all her willpower to turn and leave the room.

As she walked away her breathing was coming quickly, her heart pounding. And he wanted her close? How the hell was she going to protect herself from him if she was going to be with him every waking—and non-waking—moment?

IT WAS a night flight to the States. Ruby tried to stay awake as long as possible but the drone of the plane, together with the drone of Jamal as he talked business to Amir, combined to drive her to sleep. She was awoken by a soft touch to her cheek. She shifted around and felt a mohair blanket tickle her chin. It must have been that. Then she opened her eyes to see Amir walk away from her. She pushed herself up in her seat. They were quite alone now. Just the two of them at opposite ends of the cabin—except he'd walked over and covered her with a blanket. The tenderness of that gesture shot to the heart of her.

"Amir!" she said softly.

He stopped and turned around. "Yes?"

"Thank you. For the blanket."

He shrugged. "The pilot has turned down the temperature. I thought you might be cold."

She nodded. The fact he'd thought about her at all stunned her. "A little, maybe." But less now that she'd felt his touch against her cheek.

"You missed dinner. Are you hungry?" he asked.

She shook her head.

"You must eat properly."

Ah, of course, he was keeping his insurance warm and well fed. That was all.

"I am. I had lunch."

"Okay." He opened the drinks cabinet. "Would you care for a drink?"

"Sure. Thanks."

"Do you still like brandy? I seem to remember you used to enjoy a good Remy Martin."

Her mind shot back to her student apartment when Amir had turned up with a hamper of food, wine and good brandy.

"You developed my taste for only the best."

"So it's as well I only have the best of everything on my plane."

She pushed off the blanket and stood up and stretched, then walked across to the small bar. She took the glass from him, swirled the golden liquid around the brandy balloon and inhaled. It made her eyes water so she closed them and took a sip. It trickled down her throat like fire. And she needed fire because wasn't it fire with which you fought fire?

He propped himself against a bar stool and looked at her thoughtfully. He poured himself a stiff drink. "You are not the only one who should apologize."

She met his gaze.

"I am sorry for what happened after the party. It was outrageous. I never do things like that. I don't know what came over me."

"I do."

"Then maybe you'll explain it."

"It was always the same, Amir. Don't you remember? We could never keep our hands off each other. Nothing's changed."

"You're right. As I look at you now, I imagine you stripped of your fine clothes. I imagine you naked and my mouth exploring you."

She sucked in a deep breath and turned away with a muttered expletive. "Not anymore. I can't do that anymore."

"Why not? You've admitted you feel the same way." He took another measured sip of his drink. He flexed his fingers around the cut-glass tumbler. She could feel the effort it was taking him to be honest about his feelings. It was like watching a ten-ton truck do a U-turn at speed. She could almost smell the burning. The notion made her smile, made her determined to meet his honesty with her own.

"I have, and I do. But that's sex. It got us nowhere five years ago and there's more riding on things now. Like Hani, like our future."

"You do see a future, then."

"Of course. I'm not going to run away again, no matter what happens."

He frowned. "What do you expect to happen?"

She swallowed and looked into her glass. She hadn't wanted this conversation yet. But how could they move forward without it?

"What do you expect to happen?" he repeated, in a quieter voice.

She bit her lip and looked up into his eyes which had lost their usual arrogance. He wanted to know, she suddenly realized.

She knocked back her drink, appreciating the fire that trailed down her throat and hit her stomach, hard. She turned to him.

"Give me some food, and I'll tell you." She grinned. She'd had a small lunch and was depriving herself of food out of habit.

He went to the door.

She listened to the murmured exchange and jumped up and walked around the small cabin, noting the photos and the expensive ornaments and objects. She picked up a photo of Amir, Mia and Hani. Hani looked happy she thought, with a wrench to her gut. Then she looked at Mia and Amir. Both had imperious looks as they posed for the photograph.

He took the photograph from her, frowned and replaced it carefully on the sideboard.

"Why the frown?" she asked.

"Because things have changed so suddenly." He looked at the photo again. "Things were normal then."

"Is it normal to look as if you're counting the seconds before you can return to whatever it was you were doing?"

He shrugged. "Yes. Mia and I were busy people."

"Right." She must have conveyed something of her doubts in the tone of her voice.

He raised an eyebrow. "She was CEO of a charity for children," he said in a cooler tone. "She was very efficient and raised a lot of money for the charity. She gave it an international profile."

"Oh." Damn, she thought. Why couldn't the woman have been a freeloader, someone vacuous and, well, not good.

"She was a good woman." She looked up at him. Had he read her thoughts?

"I'm sure." She lied.

"She married me and took on a child she knew I'd fathered while our families had been discussing our union."

"Union," she said. She gave him a brief smile. "Sounds like a business merger."

"You know that that was exactly what it was. Our countries are a business. And we need to treat it like one. Especially after my father's sudden death. Things happened quickly then. They had to."

"But how did Hani fit into all this? Weren't you criticized by your people for Mia not being Hani's mother?"

"You really don't read the papers, do you, Ruby? He was born eight months after we married. A period of seclusion, a certain amount of paying people off, and Hani became both my natural child and Mia's. And that was how the world saw him."

"It was how I saw him. Because you're wrong, I did check. Maybe not the papers, but Twitter and Facebook. You protected him well. I didn't even realize he had blond hair."

"That was intentional."

She grunted as she was suddenly aware of how much had been done to keep her ignorant that her son was being raised as his and Mia's.

Her eyes lingered on Hani. "He looks happy," she conceded.

"He was. Whatever her shortcomings, she was a good mother. She gave Hani what he needed."

"And what was that?" She couldn't prevent an edge from entering her voice. She knew it wasn't fair, wasn't rational, but emotions were like that.

"Stability."

She nodded slowly. "Stability," she repeated, giving him a wan smile. "Not one of the things I'm known for."

"You don't have to keep comparing yourself to Mia."

"I can't help it, because that's what you're doing."

"I'm not, you know."

"Really?"

"No. I'm nothing if not logical, you should know that," he said, his lips tweaking with self-deprecating humor. "If Mia brought stability, you bring energy and fun."

"Sounds pretty shallow next to stability."

"I'd have agreed a month ago. But, after having seen Hani transformed in your presence, I realize that it's not shallow, it's necessary. As is stability. *That* must continue."

She shook her head. "I can't be stable. I can't do that."

"Why not?"

She sucked in a short sharp breath. "It's a long story."

"We've a long flight."

She didn't speak immediately. He rose, and for a moment she wondered if he was going to simply walk away, forget the intimacy of the moment and the invitation to hear her story. And suddenly she wanted to tell him.

"Don't go!"

He continued to the phone. His command was brief and to the point. He replaced the phone and turned to her with a wry look. "I'm not going anywhere. Simply ordering more food. I thought I'd join you." He didn't move to her immediately. Just stood as his gaze swept over her.

She tucked her bare legs under her and wriggled back into the cushions.

"What is it?"

He shook his head, as if trying to rid it of a notion. He turned his back to her and refilled their drinks, and poured a glass of water. He brought them over and placed them on the table.

"You..." He didn't meet her eyes. "You look so vulnerable, somehow. Without your armor of bright clothes, high heels and immaculate hair and make-up. It doesn't help."

"Help?"

"Help me to stay angry with you."

"Good. I'm glad. If we're going to be together for Hani, then we've got to rid ourselves of the anger." She took a sip and met his eyes, before averting them again and replacing the glass on the table. "I think my story may help there, too."

"You're not tired?"

"A little but I have trouble sleeping."

He frowned. "You never used to. I remember you spent a lot of time in bed." He smiled at the memory.

"Yes, but not much of it sleeping." She joined his smile but suddenly their smiles froze as they locked into each other's gaze. Neither spoke for long seconds. It was Ruby who looked away first. "Anyway," Ruby continued, "I hear you pacing at night, and talking on the phone. When do you sleep?"

"I don't need much sleep."

Her eyes scanned his face, taking in the dark shadows beneath his eyes. "But you look tired."

He shrugged. "One learns to live with it."

"One learns to live with many things."

He sat down opposite her. "And what have you learned to live with?"

She took a long sip of her drink before placing it carefully onto the table. "Many things. But there's some things I haven't learned to live with."

He sat back. "Such as?"

"Being alone."

He frowned. "Why?"

She shrugged and gave a smile that didn't settle, but fluttered on her lips, betraying her nerves. "It's complicated."

"What isn't?" He drank his brandy and contemplated her once more. "Tell me."

She sighed. "When I'm alone I'm afraid I…"

"You?"

"Will become like my mother."

"Your mother?" His frown deepened. "I don't understand. You've never told me about your mother."

"She"—she sucked in a deep breath—"suffered from depression. That's a mild word for what she suffered." Suddenly after what seemed a lifetime of not telling anyone, the words began to tumble out. "After I had Hani I had a taste of what she'd suffered. I don't want another one. So I avoid being on my own and I avoid hospitals. Just the smell of them takes me straight back to those days." She shook her head and gripped the glass tightly. His eyes strayed to her hands. It seemed nothing escaped his notice.

"So you fill up your days—"

"And nights—"

"With noise, because you're scared you'll become depressed if you're on your own."

She nodded. "Stupid, isn't it?"

"There's nothing logical about illness. So that would

explain all the partying."

She nodded slowly, looking into her drink. "It would."

Before she realized what he was doing, he reached out for her hand and held it tight within his. "You'll never be alone again, Ruby. You need to know that. After all, you live in a palace. There is always someone there. There's no need to be afraid anymore."

"I may not be alone, but I have the hospital to come. But I'm guessing the blood transfusion shouldn't entail an overnight stay for me. So I should just about cope with that."

Slowly he withdrew his hands. He didn't reply, and her heart sank.

"Shouldn't I?"

"Ruby, I…"

She shivered. "I'm cold." She jumped up, not wanting to hear what he was having trouble putting into words. Here, flying high above the Atlantic, she wasn't sure she could cope with bad news. "I think I'll go to bed now after all." She walked over to the door, grasped the door handle and suddenly stilled. Slowly she turned to face him. "You're not telling me everything, are you?"

He shook his head. "No."

"And… I still shouldn't be afraid?" His silence was an answer in itself. She grunted, and went out the door, into the bedroom. She leaned back against the door, wondering what the hell she'd gotten herself into.

AMIR PRESSED his eyes tight shut. But it didn't stop him from seeing her eyes, wide and scared. And it cut through to a heart he'd thought was gone.

He'd told her there was no need to be afraid. And there was.

He'd told himself he had no feelings for her. And he had.

CHAPTER 8

She awoke to find herself alone. Despite what Amir had said, he was nowhere to be seen in the private section of the plane. It was only after she'd showered and dressed and eaten breakfast alone, that she'd ventured out to find his office, close to the pilot's cockpit, where he was hard at work with Jamal and a secretary. They all looked up as she entered the room. They didn't look welcoming.

She gave a tentative smile. "Good morning," she ventured.

The two assistants inclined their heads in a pale imitations of the version of the bow they gave to their king and sheikh. Amir rose from his seat and met her gaze.

"You wanted something?" Amir asked.

She swallowed, determined to face down the stern glances from Amir and his assistants. "Yes. I'd like a word."

"I'm busy at the moment." He glanced at the desk laden with papers. "After we land we can have a meeting if you wish." He sighed, as if annoyed at having to indulge a nuisance.

"A meeting," she repeated, a spark of anger giving her strength. "As in a limited time during which we sit and talk."

"I'm glad you understand the definition of the word meeting. Now, as you can see I'm busy—"

"Perhaps you'd like me to prepare an agenda."

He resumed his scanning of a document Jamal had pushed in front of him. "An excellent idea."

The spark turned into a wicked flame which licked at her mind and heart. "Would you like me to take the minutes as well?"

A muscle flickered in his jaw as his face stiffened. His assistants looked from one to the other, and carefully avoided looking at her. Amir drew in a deep breath and closed the folder, and pushed it to Jamal. "Please leave us for five minutes."

Ruby stood aside to let the assistants out of the office. As soon as the door was closed she folded her arms. "What's going on, Amir?"

He indicated the work. "What do you think, Ruby? I'm working. And you're interrupting my work." He sighed and sat back. "This had better be important."

She pressed her lips together in an attempt to suppress the first thing that came to mind which she knew wouldn't get her anywhere. Swearing never did. She walked over to the table, sat in one of the vacated seats, and leaned forward on folded arms so he couldn't avoid her gaze.

"It is, Amir, it is."

"Proceed, then."

"You said to me that you weren't telling me everything. Correct?"

He blinked but otherwise his expression didn't change. "Correct," he murmured.

"Unsurprisingly, I'd like to know what exactly it is that you're *not* telling me."

"Don't you think I'd have told you if I considered it a good idea?"

117

"*I* will be the judge of that, thank you. Whatever it is you're keeping from me affects me, and it affects my son. I have a right to know."

His eyes probed hers for a moment, before he gave her a brief nod.

"Okay. You were right about the blood transfusion. I didn't need your blood. I didn't want your blood. I could get that elsewhere."

She swallowed. "Then... what made you change your mind?"

He cleared his throat and her fears upped a notch. "Your hospital records showed—"

"How the hell did you get hold of those?"

"By paying the right people."

She grunted. She didn't doubt it. "So, what did they show?"

"That your kidney would be a match for Hani."

It was as if lightning had struck, casting them both immobile. The noise of the plane seemed to magnify around them. She swallowed. "And why... would that be of interest?"

"Some months ago the consultant informed me that Hani might need a kidney transplant."

She sat back as if punched. "My kidney. You need my kidney for a transplant." She sank her head into her hands as panic raged within at the thought of the operation, and a fall into the abyss of depression which would surely follow.

"But the consultant's reports have been cautiously optimistic," he said.

She looked up and shook her head in confusion. "Meaning?"

"The last set of results showed the new drugs are working better than expected. If that continues, a transplant won't be required. I didn't see the point in telling you something which might not happen."

Relief exploded within her. "That's what you do with a child, not an adult. You should have told me everything. How about starting now?"

He nodded. "Hani started on these new drugs two months ago. As I say, the results have been extremely promising. I'm speaking to the consultant again later today."

She sighed and gave Amir a brief smile. "So, good news so far then."

"Yes. We'll know for definite by the end of today."

"One thing I don't understand."

"Yes?"

"If you knew the treatment was going well, why did you need me?"

"Insurance."

The cold clinical word stung.

"Of course. I was simply insurance against Hani's deterioration. Or rather my kidney was, because it wasn't me you wanted, was it?"

"Ruby, you gave our son up for adoption! No, I didn't want someone who could do that. And no, I didn't want my son anywhere near a mother who could do that!"

She rose, and the blood drained from her body. Stars burst in her eyes and she clutched the back of the chair, wondering if she was going to faint. Then the moment passed and she stepped away.

"You're never going to forgive me, are you?"

He narrowed his eyes, as if struck by her question. "Does it matter?"

"To me, it does. And you haven't answered my question. Are you ever going to forgive me?"

In the pause that followed she felt like their future happiness depended on it.

"I wish to God I could." His tone was bleak, his expression bleaker.

She left the cabin without a backward glance and took her seat once more by the window. She looked out over the clouds and blue sky at the ruffled sea far below. She'd explained everything to him. There was nothing more she could do apart from accept the fact that there would always be this barrier between them.

They'd be reaching Boston soon, and Hani. She might not have any kind of emotional future with Amir, but she'd be seeing her son soon. But as she visualized him, the picture fragmented as she suddenly realized that, if her kidneys were no longer required, then neither was she.

RUBY HAD FORGOTTEN what autumn in Massachusetts was like. All flaming hues of oranges, russets and reds with brilliant blue skies and a nip in the air she hadn't felt in a long time. She had much to be thankful for, she reminded herself. The fact that Hani's prognosis was better now than it had ever been, and the fact that she was in his life. For now, at least.

She had a lot to be thankful for, she repeated to herself as she glanced at Amir, who sat beside her in the rear of the limousine, his phone glued to his ear, talking one moment in Arabic, the next in English. He hadn't stopped since the moment he'd got into the car. One call had followed another as he continued the business of ruling a country which never slept.

Ruby turned to gaze out the window once more. Amir had hardly glanced at her since they'd left the airport. It was as if he'd shut down, turned his back on their previous intimacy, as if it had never happened. Perhaps he wished it hadn't.

He continued barking orders in Arabic as the car pulled

up outside the Beacon Hill address he'd rented for the period of Hani's treatment. Ruby had only ever walked around the area, soaking up its Victorian charm, its cobblestones, brick exteriors and old-fashioned lampposts, but had never been inside one of the houses. Her crowd weren't part of the established wealth of such an area as Beacon Hill, which had the priciest real estate in Boston. She'd always hung out at the downtown warehouse loft apartments, photographic studios, and restaurants and nightclubs in the same area. This, she thought, getting out of the car and looking up at the exterior of the house, was something else.

The house had the typical red-brick exterior and flight of shallow steps up to a column-guarded deep red front door. She looked up to see Hani's face pressed against an upstairs window. Her heart stopped at his pallor.

She felt a hand on her back. Amir pocketed his phone. "The consultant says he's doing well, and not to worry about his pallor," he said.

She licked her lips and waved up at Hani, thankful and surprised by Amir's perceptive comment. "When will you receive the final results from the consultant?" she asked, her eyes fixed on the young boy whose grin split his face, before he left the window.

"By end of the day. All should be clear then."

She blinked lightly and bit her lip. With all of her heart she wanted Hani to be well, to live a long and happy life. But if that were the case, then he'd be living it away from her. Because she knew Amir enough to know that he wouldn't willingly live with someone who he couldn't forgive for their betrayal of him, and their son. And she couldn't blame him, because she couldn't forgive herself.

They might be married, but it had only been a private civic ceremony. The news was being kept a closely guarded secret it seemed. She knew that it was traditional in his

country for the civic ceremony to precede the public coronation in which he formally presented his new queen to his
country. But usually it was mere days, not weeks between the
two. She hadn't asked when it would happen and she
suspected now that it might never happen. It would be far
easier to either annul the private civic ceremony, or divorce
and pretend it had never happened.

Suddenly the front door of the house burst open and
Hani came running down the steps and into Amir's arms.
Amir didn't swing him easily, though, but carefully absorbed
Hani's energy and lifted him high, and then brought him to
him in a warm hug.

Ruby had never seen Amir give such an encompassing
hug, holding him tight against his body for a moment as he
closed his eyes. It warmed her heart, but also saddened her
because she couldn't be a part of it.

Amir set him down on the ground, and Hani turned to
Ruby and hugged her around the waist. It hadn't the passion
of Amir's hug, but it was warm and that was enough for her.
She bobbed down, and swept his hair from his face.

"Hani! It's good to see you!" she said.

"It's great to see you, too, Ruby!" Hani glanced from Ruby
to his father. After Amir smiled and nodded, he took both
their hands. "Come on and I'll show you my playroom. I
went shopping and we bought some real cool toys. And Baba
said if I'm not too tired we can have a family trip to the park."

Ruby raised an eyebrow at Amir and caught a brief eye
roll, from which he quickly recovered.

"I did," said Amir with a slow smile, which turned out to
be infectious as first Hani smiled, then Ruby, and the smiles
turned to laughter. Any doubts Ruby had about her future
with these two were pushed firmly to the back of her mind.
She had *now*. She was used to enjoying the *now*. She could do
this.

As Ruby settled down onto one of the comfortable leather sofas in the designer family room, and watched Hani show Amir his new toys, she couldn't help feeling that it was less the toys, and more the fact that this place wasn't a palace, but a real home, that had so charmed Hani, and made him appear more relaxed.

The house, while conventional on the outside, on the inside was a mixture of modern—with its state-of-the-art discrete offices and communication center—and traditional, built with a family in mind.

The three of them, Amir, Hani and Ruby, were left alone the rest of the morning—playing and chatting, while Ruby made some lunch—declining help from Amir's staff. For once, she wanted them to be alone. It might be pretense, she thought, but it felt good.

After lunch, while Hani rested, Amir returned to work, and Ruby was free to wander around the house. She pulled on a loose pullover and stepped outside into the garden. It was fresh outside, but not yet cold. Winter was creeping in slowly to the eastern seaboard this year.

Being in such an historic area, the garden was small and surrounded by brick walls, one of which was a living wall of moss. The others were either disguised with ivy, or birch trees whose leaves provided a blaze of color against the ever-green of the ivy and the old brick walls. Beneath the canopy of leaves was a strip of grass with over-sized pots containing late blooms, as well as water features at both ends, reminiscent of the pool and courtyards at the palace. Ruby wondered if it was that which had made Amir rent the house.

She sat on one of the wrought iron seats, dusted with leaves, and looked up at the building. The dark-paned windows added a modern touch to the traditional home. She sighed, and sipped the coffee she'd brought out with her. This place was a million miles from her life in Italy, or the life Amir and Hani lived in Janub Havilah. It was a life she'd never dared dream of. A life with a family. A *real* life. She'd been brought up on the outside of such a life, looking in. She'd always be the last in her group of friends to want to go home because that's when the problems began for her. That's when she'd ceased to be a child and had to make sure her mother was cared for. She'd loved her mother and she had done her best for her, but the thought of her old life on the edge of an isolated English village, never ceased to create a chill in her soul.

She drained the cup and stood up, not liking where her thoughts strayed. She'd take it moment by moment, living in the present, as she'd always done. Perhaps then this feeling of dread which reared up in her subconscious, taunting her, sickening her that it would pounce, would leave her. She glanced at her watch. Time to go. She had a family outing to attend.

BOSTON'S PUBLIC GARDENS—AS Victorian as Beacon Hill—across from the Common, were glorious at that time of year. Apart from the brilliant autumnal tones of the trees and shrubs, the late-blooming roses and other flowers added to the vivid palette of colors, as if underlining Ruby's happiness.

"So, what do you want to do first, Hani?" asked Ruby.

Hani grinned at Ruby. "The swan boats. But only if Baba allows it." His happy face suddenly clouded with doubt as he looked at his father.

Ruby had to suppress a laugh at Amir's expression. The great sheikh and king of Havilah riding a swan boat on the lagoon didn't quite fit somehow. She decided to cut him some slack.

"How about you and I ride the swan boat. That way your Baba can take some photos of us."

"Yes!" Hani jumped as he responded. "Yes, if that's all right with Baba?"

Amir shot Ruby a thankful look. "Of course. Great idea."

It was just as well Ruby had some cash to buy the rides. It seemed it had slipped Amir's mind again, and Ruby really didn't want his security guards, whom he'd agreed to keep at a distance, to come forward and spoil the illusion of family.

As the driver pedaled the swan boat out into the lagoon, Ruby glanced back at Amir who sat on a bench watching them. His security guards were easy to spot from the water—scattered around the park, their burly presence, watchful gaze, and mutterings into their mouthpieces easily signifying their occupation. It might have been irksome to anyone else, she thought, looking back at Hani, whose grin never left his face, but to her, it was a reassuring presence, a barrier to her fears.

Hani began to chat more easily as the boat slowly made its way along the centre of the main lagoon. The footbridge was crowded with people watching. Hani waved excitedly at them, and Ruby joined him. Then he turned and waved at Amir who was now walking along the footpath, keeping abreast with them. From time to time, Amir stopped and snapped photos of them on his phone, before slipping it back into his pocket and continuing along the path.

At one point a duck squawked as it flew right past them, making Hani jump and them both laugh. She turned to see Amir looking at his phone with a smile. He must have just taken a photo and was studying his phone. He was framed by a weeping willow tree and the brilliant crimson of a Japanese maple behind him. To one side was a traditional lamp. But it wasn't the setting—now matter how picture perfect it was—it was his expression. She'd never seen him in such an unguarded moment. She quickly raised her camera to her eye—her years in the modeling business had created an interest in photography which a phone camera didn't fulfill —zoomed in and clicked the shutter, before turning her attention to Hani once more.

Without prompting, Hani slipped his hand through hers as they came off the boat and were met by Amir.

They walked over the suspension style bridge, the grand columns topped by lamp globes, and along a winding path, back toward Beacon Street. The city towers soared above the trees.

They arrived at a corner where children clambered over some duckling statues. Hani ran off to do the same thing. Small statues of ducks were ranged along the brick path, wearing brightly colored hats. The mother—Mrs Mallard— led her eight ducklings, and Hani climbed on top of her, after another kid jumped down.

Ruby needed no invitation to join him and with their heads pressed together, they posed for yet another photo.

Amir slowly lowered his camera but his gaze moved from Hani—who was already slipping off the statue to check out the ducklings—and remained locked on Ruby.

Ruby felt her own smile slip as she returned to Amir's side.

"You look serious," she said, with a brief smile.

"You've accused me of *always* being serious."

She answered Amir's slight quirk of the lips with one of her own. "I reserve the right to amend my accusation."

"Now *you're* sounding serious."

She shrugged. "I can be, you know."

He slipped his arm around her. "I didn't, but I'm getting to."

She drew in a shivering breath, feeling the sexual tension flowing from him to deep inside of her. The distance which had been between them on the plane and on the car ride to the house had disappeared now. At some point in the afternoon—whether it was in the house over lunch, or in the park —Amir's disapproval of her had been forgotten. Forgotten, she reminded herself, *temporarily* forgotten. It would return, she knew that. But for now, his arm was around her and it was all she could do to keep her hands off him, and she suspected, if the look in his eyes was anything to go by, that he felt the same.

"I think," he said, "it's time we returned." His words were like a caress. He looked at Hani, who was chatting easily with another child by the duckling statues. "He mustn't overdo it."

Ruby was brought up sharp. What was she thinking? He was only being careful about Hani. He had no intention of revisiting their earlier intimacy.

With Hani's brief attempt at staying there denied with one short command from his father, they returned to the house. They were quieter than when they'd set out. Hani, because he was tired, but Amir? Ruby hadn't the first clue what Amir was thinking. But she suspected she'd soon find out.

IT WAS late in the evening when Amir put down the phone from the consultant and found, to his horror, that he was crying. He jumped up and swiped away the tears viciously. He hadn't wept since he was a child. He'd been forced to harden up and couldn't remember anything that had got to him so profoundly as his love for his child. His love for Ruby had been sealed off in a lead coffin, cauterized by his anger for a woman with so few scruples, morals or feeling. But now, as he stood, blinking by the window, not seeing the blaze of colors in the park opposite, or the passersby, gawping up at the Victorian mansions, he felt something shift inside of him.

It shouldn't have, he knew that. Nothing had changed with regard to what she'd done to him and Hani all those years ago. But it seemed his heart didn't know that. The floodgates to his emotions had been well and truly lifted and he found himself filled with feelings which for years he'd denied.

The phone call had come later than he'd hoped, and Ruby and he had spent the evening avoiding each other's gaze, jumping at the sound of a phone, and confusing Hani by their lack of attention.

The consultant had always been cautious, which was even more telling now that she'd told Amir the latest results from the new drug Hani had been taken. He hadn't realized how much stress he'd been carrying until the consultant uttered those words… "He's cured". Amir swallowed and raked his fingers through his hair.

Hani was in bed now and the house was quiet. So there was only one thing on his mind. Ruby. He left the office and the pile of papers he should be attending to, the emails he should be responding to, and the phone calls he'd yet to return. They could wait. He had to find Ruby.

It didn't take long. She was in the snug watching some nonsense on the TV. The thick drapes were closed on the dark night and her hair was bright against the black leather settee.

"Ruby," he said, as he closed the door behind them. But she made no move.

He walked around the couch to find her curled up, her eyes closed, fast asleep, her camera on her lap. He sat beside her and lifted the camera from her lap in an attempt to make her more comfortable. Her eyes shot open instantly.

"Amir!" she said, pushing herself up.

She moved her hair from her eyes and he wished his hands had done it. He wanted to touch her soft cheeks more than anything, it would seem. He craved her.

"I didn't mean to wake you," he said, knowing that wasn't strictly true.

"That's okay. It's probably just a touch of jet lag." Her eyes fell to the camera, and then back to him. She reached out for it, and reluctantly he handed it back to her.

"Looking at anything in particular?"

She fiddled with the camera and hesitated. "Yes."

"Like what?"

She looked up and his stomach clenched with desire. Her blue eyes were darker in the subdued light, like pools of water into which he wanted to dive. He swallowed.

"Like you." She brought the camera around so he could see. And he did see, but he didn't recognize the face of the man she'd captured. That man was looking closely at something. Whatever it was he was looking at had opened his lips softly, and softened the small lines around his eyes. There was a light in the eyes, too. It was him. "And I couldn't help wondering," she continued, "what it was *you* were looking at."

He knew exactly what he was looking at. "You," he said simply.

She cocked her head to one side in question.

All it took was to reach out to her and do what he'd wanted to do as he'd looked at the photo of her, and draw his finger down the side of her face, feeling the silky undulations of the eye, the cheekbone, and the jaw before he swept up and touched her lips.

"You," he repeated. Before she could open those beautiful lips to speak, he leaned in and kissed her. It was a gentle kiss, but she gasped and he pulled away. He drew in a deep calming breath. "I'm sorry, I—"

"Don't!" she said.

"No, I won't again. It's only you were…" He trailed off and shrugged.

"No," she shook her head fiercely, her eyes now blazing. "No! You misunderstand. I mean, don't stop."

He smiled at her need, because it was like his own. "But I must. I have something to tell you. About Hani. The consultant has only good news for me. The drugs are working. He should need no other treatment."

She closed her eyes and fell back against the sofa, blinking up at the ceiling rose, her gaze far away, as she gulped. Then she looked back at him sharply. "You're sure?"

"As sure as we can be. So no invasive treatment for Hani… or for you."

He watched as a tear leaked from her eye. She squeezed them shut and pinched the bridge of her nose with her fingers. He put his arm around her, and she turned her face to him, but not to talk. Her mouth sought his with an intensity he understood. The relief at Hani, the undercurrents of their lust, culminated in a passion that was hard to deny, but not impossible.

He pulled away "As much as I want you, I want to talk with you more. This changes everything."

She fiddled with her fingers for a moment before looking up at him, her expression uncharacteristically hurt. She usually hid such reactions from him. It seemed the unexpected news of Hani's recovery had knocked them both for six.

The hurt was followed by incredulity, quickly followed by a flicker of pain, worse than hurt. "Tell me, Amir, straight, what exactly does this change?"

CHAPTER 9

*R*uby watched him stride across to the window, look out at nothing, his brows knitted, and then stride back again. Whatever it was that had changed he was having a hard time trying to find words to convey it.

Her heart sank a little further. She hadn't thought her heart could sink any lower but then he turned to face her and the look in his eyes said it all. He hadn't wanted to marry her five years earlier, he hadn't wanted to marry her when she'd came back into his life, and he certainly had no reason to continue to be married to her now. Her future with Hani had just slipped through her fingers.

She jumped up, raked her fingers through her hair and twisted away from him. She couldn't bear to hear his words of finality, ending the life she'd began to actually believe in.

She picked up her phone from the table. "It's late. Maybe we should postpone this talk." She took a deep breath and then faced him, trying to focus as steadily as she could, determined to get the message across to him. The truth. "Hani is well and that's the greatest gift we could be given." She gave an awkward shrug. "Anything after that can be managed."

She paused, hoping he might stop her, say something, anything, to break the train of thoughts his silence had created.

He only nodded.

"Then I'll go to bed. We can talk in the morning… if you want to." She walked to the door, the anger mounting in her that, after all they'd shared over the past weeks, he'd turn his back on it, on her, on their future together.

She gripped the door handle and hesitated. Still he hadn't said anything. The only sound was the wind in the trees and the clatter of branches against a window, as if someone wanted to gain entry. Cars passed by outside and they could hear shrieks of laughter coming from the park.

"You'll never forgive me, will you, Amir?" she said between gritted teeth.

"Forgive you?"

With her hand still tight around the door handle, she turned to him, the anger, frustration and rejection bursting forth. "You can't forgive the fact I gave up our son."

"No, I can't."

She swung her head back to face the door. "Then, there's little more to be said." She twisted the handle, but before she could open it he'd strode across the room and placed a hand over hers.

She looked into his unreadable dark eyes. She tried to pull away but he continued to hold on.

"Where are you going?"

She tried to summon a smile. "To bed. To sleep," she added, in case he was in any doubt.

He nodded. "I can't help it, Ruby. I can't help being unable to forgive you. It's how I feel."

"And this is how *I* feel. I told you what happened, I hoped you'd understand but it doesn't look as if you do."

"It's…" He hesitated. "Complicated."

She felt cheated by the easy word. "It's not simple, that's for sure." She tried to twist the door handle again, suddenly anxious to be away from him. Because when she was with him, she felt how he saw her, and began to see herself in the same light. The kind of woman who'd give away her child. She knew there was her depression, she knew that her so-called friend had encouraged it to happen. At the time she'd thought her friend had been trying to look out for her. But, it turned out, the only person she'd been looking out for was herself by confessing all to Amir in return for cash. She knew all of these extenuating circumstances, but the bottom line was she'd given up her son and Amir would never forgive her.

She tried again to turn the handle but his grip tightened over hers.

"Please, hear me out," he said.

She shook her head. "There's no point. I can't listen to you telling me what a terrible woman I am, over and over." She swallowed back the tears. "I can't do it anymore."

She felt his breath against her cheek as he leaned into her, and his arm came around her. "You're wrong."

She huffed a laugh. "Of course I am. I'm a terrible mother, and I'm always wrong." She shot him a sideways glance. "So let me go."

"Not before you hear me out." He released his hand from hers and stepped away. "I apologize. I'm accustomed to getting my own way. Please, Ruby, will you stay, have a drink, while I try to explain something to you."

She closed her eyes for a few second. Could she sit quietly and sip a drink while he told her that there was no longer any need or desire for her to be in his or Hani's lives anymore?

"Please," he repeated, in that lowered, seductive voice which made her skin tingle and her legs weak. Damn.

"Just one drink, then."

There was something in his sigh which made her realize that he hadn't been as sure as he'd appeared. She sat on the couch, the table firmly between her and him, and folded her arms defensively. She watched as he walked over to the sideboard and poured two drinks. He placed ice in the whiskies and hesitated as he swirled the clinking ice cubes around the glass. The cut crystal glittered under the sidelight. When he turned around she immediately averted her gaze, unable to meet the dark eyes which withheld so much from her.

He handed her the drink and she took a sip as he seated himself in a single chair opposite her, as if they were strangers. Intimate strangers.

"I owe you an explanation," he said. "You might still be angry that I can't forgive you, but the explanation may go some way to helping you to understand me."

She nodded and took another nervous sip of her whiskey, unable to imagine what he was about to tell her. "Okay. I'm listening."

He looked up as if seeking inspiration, as if unsure, and sighed before returning his gaze to hers once more. "I haven't told anyone what I'm about to tell you."

She angled her head to one side. "Okay. Well, I hope you know me well enough to know that I won't repeat it."

"I do know, *and* trust that much."

She didn't like how his trust in her was so limited. "Well, I guess that's something."

"It is, believe me. Look, it's difficult, what I'm about to say. I haven't talked about it to a soul."

"Not to Mia?"

"No, not even Mia."

"But you will to me? Why?"

"Because I owe you an explanation. I kept Hani from you

when I knew you were looking for him. And I regret that, and I want you to know why."

The memory of those years chasing lawyers, red herrings, trails that went cold and ended with her lost in a crowd, as she tried to drown her sorrows in company, swept over her, leaving her with the same feelings of desolation and resentment. "Good, because I'd like to know why."

"I hated that you adopted Hani out. I hated it." The vehemence and feeling lingered on the air. She almost recoiled under the passion of feeling.

"I didn't much like it either. But, as I explained, I wasn't in my right mind at the time. And there hasn't been a moment that I haven't regretted it afterwards. You have to believe that."

"I do. But, you know, some hatreds—like adoption—go deeper than rational thought. Some feelings can never be addressed, they're so ingrained."

"You mean you were born with an ingrained hatred for adoption?" She had no idea where he was going with this. "Really?"

"Something like that."

"Tell me, what it's like—*exactly*." Her heart thumped heavily. She needed to understand this inexplicable man whom she loved but continued to feel distant from.

"Few people know."

"I'd like to be one of those people."

He hesitated, searching her face for an answer she didn't even know the question to. "My mother was pregnant when she discovered my father had a preference for one particular brothel."

Ruby sat back in her chair in shock. "What? But, your father was, was so... Well, of course, I didn't know him, but his reputation was..." She trailed off, as she tried to recall his impression through the press, which from memory was entirely respectable.

"That of a man for whom family came first. And he was. Except his definition of family was obviously wider than my mother had known."

"So what happened? Did your father stop going to the brothel? You were born and then everyone ended up happily ever after?"

He carefully picked up his whiskey, swirled it around the glass, and then replaced it on the table without drinking. "Not exactly. My father continued his visits to the brothel and my mother decided to follow him one day. She found him with a beautiful woman, a prostitute. And she discovered the woman was pregnant. My father claimed it was his child."

"Jesus! That must have devastated you mother."

"It did. My mother lost the baby."

"What? But..."

"My mother miscarried her child."

"So, then... She became pregnant with you later?"

"No. She wasn't able to have any more children. But my father's mistress gave birth to a boy. By that time my father was so consumed by guilt at what had happened to my mother that he'd rejected his mistress. He was contrite. He swore to my mother that it would never happen again. But they were facing a future without sons and my mother knew my father wanted a son, that the country needed one. So she went to my father's mistress and they came to a deal. Money for a baby. Sound familiar?"

Amir's voice had become as bitter as bile. Ruby could feel the blood run from her face. "And you're that boy," she whispered, in a voice which felt like gravel. "You were adopted, just like Hani."

"No. Not just like Hani. My father simply took custody. To all the world, I'm my father and mother's natural child."

"But to you," she said bleakly, "you were always rejected by your birth mother."

He nodded. "I was nineteen years old when my father told me I was adopted. My mother was ill during the last years of her life and wasn't herself. She told me I wasn't her son. My father had no choice but to explain."

"And what was your reaction?"

"Again, complicated. I hated my father for a time and went off the rails for a few years."

"The years in which you met me."

He nodded.

She swallowed. She had to know the answer to a question she'd never had the chance to ask.

"If you hated him so much, then why did you agree to marry someone you didn't love?"

"Duty. Ultimately, he was my father and whatever my feelings, I had a duty to him."

Ruby shook her head, hardly able to absorb what Amir was telling her.

"A duty to the man who, if it hadn't been for your mother, would have let you go."

"But he didn't. It was my birth mother who let me go, who sold me."

"Right," she said softly. "Just like you believed I had. But you let me go first, Amir. You told me you didn't love me, and you walked away."

He nodded once, leaned back on the chair and closed his eyes briefly, before continuing.

"My father wanted me to marry Mia for country and family reasons. He didn't want me to make the same mistakes he had. I owed my parents my life and I had a responsibility and duty to them which I vowed I'd never shirk. My family, and my country, required it of me. Without the marriage, there would have been issues, problems between warring clans, age-old divisions which would have continued. I owed it to everyone to do what was required of me."

"Why didn't you tell me?"

"I thought it would be easier for you if I lied."

She grunted a derisive laugh. "The man of honor and duty, lying."

"I did what I thought was best. I had no choice, Ruby, you must understand that."

"We all have choices. You put duty before love—" She broke off. "At least I think you did. In the beginning you told me you loved me and I believed you. Was I wrong to do that? And then, when you broke it off and said you didn't love me, I didn't believe you. Was I wrong then too?"

The silence weighed heavily.

"You were wrong not to tell me about your pregnancy," he said at last.

His lack of direct response was telling. "Why? You'd gone from my life. Why would I want you to have anything to do with my baby, when you didn't want anything to do with me?"

"It was my duty to care for a child I fathered."

"But not your duty to care for a woman who you'd said you loved." She couldn't prevent a bitter tone from entering her voice. "And so history repeated itself. Like father, like son."

The branches of the tree outside battered against the window, driven by a stray gust of wind, as if trying to rebuke her, just as Amir rebuked her, and always would. She rolled her head to look out through an un-curtained side window. She could just see the first scattering of stars prick through the indigo sky.

"Yes," said Amir. "I felt I'd let everyone down."

"Your family, you mean."

"My family and, most especially, you. When I told you we couldn't see each other again, I said things which weren't true. It was hard but I believed you'd find it easier if you believed I didn't love you. So I told you that."

"Easier? Perhaps in some ways. In that I knew I couldn't go to you. I had no choices. If having no choices is easier, then, yes, it was. But I was pregnant and alone. I was terrified and I sunk to a depth that I hadn't imagined I could sink to."

"I'm sorry. I did what I thought best."

"We both did. But it didn't turn out a spectacular success, did it?"

He stood up. "Come on. It's time to go to bed."

She looked up at him, darkly silhouetted now against a lamp he'd lit against the darkness, and didn't move. For all the shock of the revelations, she'd shared an intimacy with Amir that she'd never shared before. Here, in the casual lounge, there was no imposing building, no priceless artifacts surrounding them, nothing to come between them. Even the past seemed to have magically been robbed of its poison by talking about it. She could sense he felt the same. The formality in his movements was gone, revealing itself in the gesture of his hand reaching out to her. At that moment he was the real Amir, the young man she'd known when they were both carefree and in love. She knew he'd retreat at some point, but for now he was here, with her in more than just body.

She rose on the balls of her feet and cupped her hands either side of his cheeks and kissed him gently on the mouth. She sighed as she rolled back onto her feet once more. He met her gaze, the whites of his eyes glowing other-worldly in the darkness.

"Ruby…" Her whispered name sounded like a sigh.

She lifted her eyes from his lips to his eyes once more and parted her lips instinctively. He brought his lips to touch hers and they barely touched before he drew away.

"Thank you for telling me, Amir. It helps."

He nodded. "It helped me, too."

She gave him a brief smile and walked to the door. The few steps seemed endless. This time he didn't try to stop her. Without a backward glance she went to her bedroom and closed the door behind her. There were no footsteps following her.

Instinctively she walked to the mirror, took off her earrings and picked up her hair brush. She shook out her hair and began pounding the brush against her head, as she went over and over what he'd just told her. And what it meant for her, and their future together.

He might never forgive her for letting their child go. And she understood that because didn't she feel the same? But at least she understood why now. And the 'why' was inextricably linked with the same 'why' behind his marriage. He'd been raised with twin values: duty to his family and his country, and a feeling of deep betrayal by his birth mother. And those values ran deep. And, because of that, she didn't know if he could love her as he'd once loved her.

She'd asked him whether he still loved her, and he hadn't answered.

Then she stopped, the hairbrush raised halfway to her head and she fixed on her gaze in the mirror. She could no longer avoid the thought which had hit her earlier—the thought she'd been repelling, ever since Amir told her that Hani was cured. If she wasn't needed any longer for insurance against Hani's health, then she'd lost her bargaining tool to stay. She was surplus to requirements.

She swallowed and re-ran her conversations with Amir, raking them for signs of commitment for the future. Love?

No. Continuing their marriage? There'd been no further talk of that.

They'd had sex, yes. Crazy, intense sex, but it seemed that was all they had.

She had to face the fact that she was no longer needed in their lives.

CHAPTER 10

The return journey to Havilah was subdued. A nurse from the clinic accompanied them, to ensure constant monitoring of Hani's health for the next few months. With the nurse in attendance, and Amir's advisors and assistants always present, she'd had the busyness she'd always craved. Except now she didn't crave it. Now she only wanted an answer to a question she dare not ask. Because if the answer was as she'd imagined, she didn't know where to go from there. She decided to try to find out the answer by listening. She didn't have to wait long for the first clue. And it came from an unexpected quarter.

She'd been sitting listening to Hani talk to the nurse. He was stronger now. She could see it in the length of time he could be active—always non-stop talking and doing—before he faded and needed a sleep. He was also tolerating different food now, enjoying things which had been forbidden for a long while.

But it wasn't until Hani ran over to show the nurse a photo, after a polite enquiry from her, that Ruby focused sharply on what was being said.

"And who's this?" asked the nurse, indulging her charge with interest she no doubt didn't feel.

"That's my mother. She was very beautiful." Tears filled his eyes and he sniffed. He swallowed and brushed the tears away with the back of his hand. "She died in a car accident."

"Oh, I'm sorry," said the nurse sympathetically, after a glance full of curiosity at Ruby, who had to look away. "But she's in heaven now, isn't she?"

Hani nodded. "Yes. Everyone says so because she was so nice and good. She loved me and I'm very sad she's not here any more, but Baba says she'll always stay in our hearts." He replaced the photo, now recovered somewhat, comforted by remembering his father's words.

Ruby stared at the magazine in front of her. The words became jumbled. Who was she trying to kid? She might be married to Amir, but Hani had a mother who'd loved him and who he continued to love, unreservedly, a mother whose memory she could never compete with. She'd lost that, given it to another. Who was she now? A wife who could be disposed of by a signature—Amir's signature.

Hani continued to look at the photo. "I miss her. No one can ever replace my mother."

The nurse didn't dare look back at Ruby, who stayed mute, her eyes downcast, as she absorbed the reality of her world. Hani had no intention of hurting her, he simply spoke from the heart. A heart that didn't want her as a mother. He wanted no one except the woman who'd adopted him and had died. How could she compete with a saint?

The rest of the journey she sat alone in the bedroom while Hani slept in another room and Amir worked in his office, surrounded by a wall of staff. As she lay on the bed—listening to the thrum of the airplane, the long, long day remaining light as they headed east—she tried desperately to work out what she could do to take control. Since the time when Hani was born and her recovery from her subsequent depression, she'd always made sure she was in control—that way she avoided the worst of the panic which dogged her.

What would she do if Amir didn't want her in his or Hani's life anymore? She couldn't tell Hani that she was his birth mother, not when he plainly adored his adopted mother. She had nothing except Amir's goodwill to allow her to stay. And she wasn't sure she even had that. Passion, yes, but anything more enduring than that? She had no idea.

SHE WAS awoken hours later by a crew member informing her they would be landing shortly. Her first reaction was panic. As she tidied herself up, she glanced at the magazine she'd been reading earlier. The feature spread was of a fashion shoot in the UK. She knew the photographer, the magazine editor it was destined for, as well as the models. She could always go back to that. But the thought of leaving Hani and Amir was too painful. For better or worse, she'd thrown in her lot with them and would have to stay to see how it ended. And she had a feeling it might be sooner rather than later.

They drove back to the palace in separate cars. No one explained this to her. She had to suppose it was because Amir was immediately swept off to the official part of the palace where he had meetings with visiting officials. Meanwhile, Ruby and Hani were left alone in the private quarters. She'd quickly given the exhausted nurse leave to rest.

She lay on the divan next to a restless Hani, watching a movie. If, she considered, she had to leave soon, at least she'd have the memories such as this and the past few weeks to sustain her. She tried to convince herself, but knew that, after such a taste, it would never be enough.

They watched one film after another with Hani dozing

from time to time. At those times, she stroked his hair and watched him, trying to imprint in her memory every line of his face, every feature, every nuanced expression which flickered across his face as he dreamed.

He awoke quickly, moving from sleep to activity in an instant. The film they'd been watching was coming to a close and there was a wedding scene.

"Who's getting married?" he asked. "Was it the people who were arguing at the beginning?"

"That's right."

"Strange that they like each other. They didn't seem to."

She ruffled his hair. "Life's like that sometimes. Other things get in the way and complicate friendships."

He considered this for a moment.

"Like what?"

"Well," she said, shifting herself to sitting. He did the same. "Like misunderstandings."

"But they can be sorted by just talking, can't they?"

Ruby didn't know where Hani got his wisdom from, but it wasn't from her. "You're right, they can. Perhaps a better example would be when a boy might love a girl, but that boy might think it's wrong for some reason."

"What kind of reason?"

She shrugged, as she thought of Amir. "Like because his parents might want him to marry someone else."

"But why would they want to do that?"

"Maybe because they move in different circles, and want someone they know, someone from their world, someone who would fit in."

"Oh," said Hani, who obviously understood this a little better.

She hesitated, but had to ask. "You said that no one could ever be your mother except Mia."

He screwed up his face and thought, then continued fiddling with something. "That's right."

"But... don't you think that—"

Suddenly there was a sound at the door and Ruby and Hani both looked up to see Amir standing at the door with a face like thunder.

"Baba!" said Hani, jumping up and running over to him. But he, too, sensed Amir's mood, and stopped short of hugging him. "I thought you were in meetings all day."

"I was. But I wanted to see how you were." He cast a disapproving glance at Ruby, before tousling his son's hair.

"I'm fine, Baba, honestly. I feel so much better than before."

"That's good. So do you think you can stay up for tonight's dinner?"

"Yes! Of course. I've been looking forward to it."

This was news to Ruby.

"Then, come along with me, I'll return you to your rooms."

Hani went into the hall and Amir was about to close the door when Ruby jumped up.

"I just wanted to say—" said Ruby.

"I think you've said quite enough already," he said, as he closed the door on her.

She sat on the sofa with her head in her hands. Amir must have heard her talking to Hani about his mother. She blushed. She imagined how it would have looked to Amir. As if she were trying to pressure Hani into loving her. Amir would hate that. But she hadn't, had she? The conversation had simply arisen from the film. But the stark facts remained. Amir had witnessed her about to ask Hani if she could ever replace Mia in his life, if he could love her. It made her look desperate. It made her look as if she were putting her own feelings above those of their son.

Amir felt an undercurrent of disquiet as he sat at the top table, surrounded with dignitaries and his son. The state banquet included the kings of his two neighboring countries, Gharb Havilah and Sharq Havilah. It was good to have their presence here, reminding him of the steadiness of his world when his own personal life seemed to be in such disarray.

He glanced along the table to where Ruby was sitting. She was seated further away from him than he'd intended but his assistant had said protocol demanded others sit nearer, and he was correct, so the seating arrangements had remained, but he could see Ruby wasn't happy about it.

Or maybe she wasn't happy about their earlier meeting. For some reason whenever he saw Ruby his famed control shredded. Especially when it involved Hani. That she should talk to Hani of his love for Mia showed she was feeling insecure, that much was obvious, and he completely understood the reason why. But he'd spent a lifetime being protective around Hani and old habits died hard. Even when it came to someone who also loved Hani with a passion.

He'd have to make it up to her. And he could think of a few interesting options which he'd explore later.

"So it's down to me," said the king of Gharb Havilah, Sheikh Zavian.

Amir frowned, momentarily confused.

"To bring peace to our countries," continued Zavian.

"You're going to bite the bullet, then," said the king of Sharq Havilah, Sheikh Roshan, with a grin. "Take one for the team. Marry the Tawazun sheikha."

Zavian cast a dark look at Roshan. "Only because your womanizing reputation makes you less appealing to her father." He grunted and pressed his joined hands to his mouth. Amir frowned. Zavian appeared uncharacteristically unsettled.

"Is anything the matter, Zavian?" Amir asked.

The cloud swiftly vanished and Zavian shook his head. "Nothing. All is as it should be." He cast a quick smile at the other two men and settled his gaze on Ruby. "And your new queen. She's very beautiful, and charming I hear. But you are keeping her away from us, Amir."

Amir met Zavian's perceptive gaze. "This is all very new to her."

"And to you, I think."

"I've been married before."

"Yes. But I haven't seen that look in your eyes before."

Amir shifted in his seat. "I don't know what you mean."

Zavain tilted his head and his stern lips quirked slightly. "Do you not?"

Amir didn't answer. He knew what Zavian was getting at. Each beat of his heart was a reminder of the love he felt for Ruby, a love which consumed his body and mind, and which he knew now would never leave. But he was also aware that it weakened him. Even now with his fellow kings, he felt that weakness which had not existed before. But it was only a weakness if he admitted it. And he had no intention of doing that, not to Zavian or Roshan, or to Ruby.

"No, I don't," he replied at last.

"Shame," said Roshan. "Such a beautiful wife should be appreciated." A slow smile spread over his face. "And publicly." He raised his glass and turned to face everyone in the room. "Raise your glasses to the beautiful new queen of Janub Havilah."

There were polite smiles as the glasses were raised and the toast repeated around the room. Ruby blushed as all eyes were fixed on her. Amir watched as she quickly recovered and gracefully nodded and smiled at everyone. She did it well. But, still, he was irritated by the handsome Roshan's attention on Ruby. And even more so when Roshan said, in a voice which reached every corner of the room.

"And are you going to tell us when the formal coronation will take place, Amir?"

Amir didn't miss a beat, his eyes never leaving Ruby's.

"No, actually Roshan. I'm not." It was none of Roshan's business, only his.

Roshan smiled, and turned to the woman to his left, unperturbed by the snub.

The blush drained from Ruby's face. He caught her gaze and nodded. Her expression wavered a little as if she didn't understand his nod. She turned away quickly, her blush lingering in her cheeks and in her averted gaze. Maybe she didn't understand but she would.

Ruby slipped away from the banquet as soon as she could. She didn't even know why she'd been invited. Stuck at the end of the table between the wife of a lowly clerk and an elderly gentleman who was half asleep, it was clear where she came in the pecking order—nowhere.

She undressed and lay in her robe on the bed, the window wide open, listening to the night sounds of the nearby desert drifting to her on the warm breeze. She preferred no air conditioning. She felt in touch with the world that way. And it was a world she'd be leaving soon. It was clear she was no longer wanted. Not by Amir, and not by Hani. Amir wanted her only for sex. His negative response to the question of her coronation at dinner couldn't have been plainer—he had no intention of continuing this sham of a marriage. And Hani wanted her for fun, for company, as if she were a fun older sister. Not a mother. And it was a mother she wanted to be. That or nothing.

She jumped up. She couldn't bear doing nothing. She'd do as Hani had suggested. She'd go to his room so they could talk, and have this out once and for all.

She went through the interconnecting door into Amir's room. It was empty, as she knew it would be. She glanced at the bed but went in the opposite direction, out onto the balcony which adjoined hers, and sat on the chair, looking into the dark night, the breeze from the desert edged with dry heat and orange blossom from the garden below.

She didn't hear the door open but she knew exactly when Amir entered the room. Something changed, in the atmosphere and within her. It was as if she had a sixth sense which detected Amir's presence inside her, before she'd seen or heard him. Or felt him, she thought, as he came behind her and slipped his hands around her shoulders, caressing them, making her close her eyes as bliss stole over her.

She breathed him in. He smelled of exotic spices, of leather, ambergris, of clean sweat and of male outdoors, of dry heat and smoke. The whole combined to create a unique scent which was his essence. It made her mouth water and her body flicker with desire again.

It almost made her forget the turbulent emotions she had for him. Anger that he had no intention of forging a life with her, humiliation that she'd believed he had, but beyond those things, pleasure that she was being touched and caressed by the man she loved.

She didn't turn around, only placed her hand on his and closed her eyes for a moment, willing herself to find the strength she needed to reject him.

"This is a nice surprise," he said.

She took his hand from her and stood up to face him.

"You think I've come for sex?"

His eyes which glittered from the outside lights, narrowed. "That sounds quite… basic."

"That's what it is, isn't it? Our relationship is quite… basic."

He brushed her hair back from her face and stood closer to her. He glanced down at her body which was naked beneath the robe. She shouldn't have undressed, she thought belatedly. She could feel her nipples harden under his gaze and the brush of his hand as he reached up for her face. He slid one hand into her hair and kissed her.

She should move, she should reject him, she should insist on talking. Instead desire heated inside her, threatening to consume her. He stopped kissing her and pulled the belt of her robe. She slammed her hand over his just in time, preventing the belt from sliding through the loop and her robe from gaping open.

He stepped back and pulled off his tie. "And is *basic* such a bad thing?"

"Not when it's a building block to something more. But alone?" She shook her head. "It's not enough to base a relationship on."

He cocked his head to one side so he could see her face.

"*Habibti*, what is the matter?"

She smoothed her hand across his chest, not meeting his gaze. "Do you doubt your ability to seduce?" she murmured.

"No. And nor do I doubt my ability to know when something's wrong. I repeat, what is the matter?"

She thrust her fingers through her hair. "You want to know what the matter is? Okay, I'll tell you. It's you, getting angry with me for talking to Hani—*our* son, not only yours—about his feelings for Mia, for me, his mother. *That* is the matter."

"I wasn't angry," he answered, in a surprisingly mild tone.

"Then why the scene?"

"Scene?"

"You threw me a black look and walked out with a word!"

He shrugged. "It took me by surprise, that's all. I'm not used to another person having such a familiar relationship with him, talking in such a personal way about me. My instinct was to reject it, but I understood."

She folded her arms. "And what did you think you understood?"

"That you're feeling insecure about our future."

Her heart beat furiously and she swallowed as anxiety rose up inside her. She paused, aware of the sound of the blood pulsing in her ears. "If I hadn't been then, I am now. When you refused to talk about my coronation at dinner, I can only come to one conclusion."

"Only one?" His lips quirked into a brief smile and she thought he was laughing at her. He didn't even take this conversation seriously. "And you accuse me of being black and white. Surely there could be other conclusions to be drawn from my silence on the subject of your coronation."

"The obvious one is that you've no wish for it to proceed."

She waited for his response, searching his face for clues as to his real feelings.

"We made an agreement, Amir," she continued, unable to stand the silence and what it might mean. "To be married—"

"And we are—"

"And to *remain* married for the sake of our son's health."

He frowned and looked away. She hated the way he did it. "But our son is now well. It's not necessary to remain together for his health." Then he returned his gaze to her and she couldn't read what lay in his eyes. But then she didn't have to read it. His words said everything.

With one sentence her life had crumbled and her fears

had re-established themselves. She swallowed. She had to keep control at least for a while longer.

"Not necessary," she repeated, and turned before she made a fool of herself with tears.

"Ruby," he said.

She walked away, proud of the fact that she'd managed to find the strength from somewhere to walk tall. Her pace quickened as she reached the door.

"Ruby," he repeated with a threatening growl. "Don't walk out on me."

Her hand clamped around the door handle of the inter-connecting door, and she paused, unable to believe he wanted to both reject her and be the one to say when she could leave. She turned to face him, not caring that her eyes glittered with tears.

"You can't have it both ways, Amir. You can't *not* want me, and stop me from leaving until you say so."

"I didn't say—"

She didn't wait around to find out what he did or didn't say. She knew what he said, and what he wanted. It was in his authoritative manner, in his anger that she dared to walk out on him, and not least, in what he'd said. There was no place in his life for a woman like her, and there was no place in Hani's life for a mother. And she couldn't bear to be anything else to him now.

So she returned to her bedroom, half-hoping that she'd hear the door open behind her and Amir emerge and plead with her to stay, beg her to forgive him and swear his undying love for her.

But as the minutes lengthened and turned into a period of time which couldn't be explained any other way, she opened her closet and threw her things onto the bed and hastily packed her suitcase. By the time she stepped out of the shower, the interconnecting door was still closed, and there was no sound coming from Amir's room. There was only silence—a silence which rose around her, blocking her from her dreams. Dreams that she'd been a fool to believe would ever become reality. Dry-eyed, she reached for her phone. She had a flight to book.

CHAPTER 11

The private wing of the palace was quiet when Ruby emerged late morning. She'd chosen that time as she knew Amir would be busy working in the main building, and Hani would be resting quietly, adhering to the old regime which Amir had instigated. Hani might be on the road to recovery but, Ruby had to admit, some of Amir's routines, such as this one, were good ones.

She gave her bedroom one last glance around before closing the door. This was no time for regret or sentiment—she had to move on, whether she liked it or not. And she didn't. But the alternative—of remaining here for as long as Amir decided he wanted her in his bed—wasn't viable. She'd be belittled in Hani's eyes—his 'fun' friend, there for as long as Amir wanted her.

She walked quickly past Amir's bedroom. He'd emerged before dawn, not stopping by her room, and hadn't returned since. He couldn't have made it any clearer. He wanted her, but not in the same way she wanted him.

She'd had her bags taken to a taxi which waited discreetly outside on the street, lost amid the sightseers and clamor of the old city which fronted the public buildings. With all the palace's visitors no one would have looked twice at the porter taking her suitcases to a taxi.

She knocked quietly on the door and peeped her head around to look inside. Hani's eyes lit up and she felt a stab of pain. She'd have to learn to live with that.

"Hi, Hani!"

"Hi, Ruby! What are you doing here?" he asked, looking up from a book. "I thought all the grown ups were at the reception. Father said they'd be, anyway."

"Ah, well, maybe just for today I'm not a grown up like they are."

"That's cool. Then you can read with me if you like."

She came and sat beside him. "I'd very much like. What are you reading?"

The Wind in the Willows.

"The Wind in the Willows?" Ruby was surprised at the old-fashioned English classic. "Really? How come?"

"I found it." He flicked over to the front of the book to reveal an inscription. "It was my grandmother's book. Baba told me that she had an English nanny who read English books to her. There's a heap still in the library."

Ruby gave a soft grunt of surprise. She hadn't known that. "And are you enjoying it?"

"Yes. My nanny read it to me before but I like re-reading some bits. Have you read it?"

"Yes, my mother used to read it to me. I used to make paper boats and float them on the stream and imagine Rat sailed in them." She picked up some paper. "I'll make you one if you like."

Hani's eyes lit up. "Yes, please!"

"Okay, if you read me your favorite bit, I'll make you a boat. Deal?"

"Deal."

After Hani finished reading to her the passage about Badger's house—his memory helping him over the more difficult words—Ruby gave him the paper boat, trying to subdue the rising poignancy his favorite passage had created. It described a house which wasn't a palace, but a home, small, cozy, quaint and full of character. A place of safety. Ruby could identify with that.

"It's beautiful," she said after a long pause.

"It makes me feel good," he said. And her heart clenched. She had to get this over with.

"Hani, I came because I have something to tell you."

He looked up at her, and blinked. "Are you leaving?"

She nearly choked on her well-rehearsed words. "Well, yes. What made you think that?"

"Ah, Baba said you wouldn't be staying for long."

"When did he say that?"

"Oh, ages ago, after you first arrived. He told me not to get too attached because you wouldn't be hanging around."

She tried to give him a smile, but nothing emerged. She was out of smiles. She stroked his hair instead and kissed his head before rising.

"Seems he was right," she said quietly, her voice hoarse. She cleared her throat.

"Not really," he said with big eyes. "Because I *am* attached. I'm going to miss you, Ruby." He said it with such calmness, as if he was used to people he was attached to leaving him, that Ruby nearly changed her mind. "You're fun," he added.

Fun. She was fun for her son, and fun for his father. But she needed more than fun. She needed to be loved. Maybe Hani did love her, it was hard to tell. He'd obviously spent his short life protecting himself from loving people in case they left. Like hired staff, like Mia had.

She kissed him again and jumped up. "I have to go. I've a taxi waiting. I'm going to England, where I was born. I have

157

work there. But I'm only a phone call away. You call me if you want to chat, right?"

"When?"

She laughed with relief. He was his father's son all right, wanting specifics. "How about tomorrow morning? I'll be in the UK by then, and I'll wish you good morning." He frowned. "What is it?"

"I'm not allowed on my computer until after breakfast."

"Then you contact me when you can." She fiddled with the handles of her bag. "And don't worry if something crops up. It's no biggie, just ring me when you fancy a chat, right?"

"Right." He jumped up and gave her a hug. No biggie, she thought. She'd never lied to her son before. Only by omission. He stepped away.

She smiled. "Make sure you have fun, Hani, even if I'm not here. Imagine me here in spirit. Like when you step into Badger's house when you want to feel nice, you can imagine the things we've done to get yourself into a fun mood, yes?"

He nodded. "We have had some fun, haven't we, Ruby?"

"We have." She swallowed and nodded, and quickly left the room. Her walk turned into a run as she followed the back corridors and servants' passages out to the rear service courtyard and through to the waiting taxi.

AMIR WAVED off the visiting dignitaries and went inside the palace, also waving away his assistants. The meeting had gone well. It seemed the diplomats from Tawazun weren't concerned who their sheikha married—him, Zavian or Roshan. He'd married Ruby on the understanding from the king of Tawazun that this was so, but the diplomats made it official.

For the first time since Ruby had returned to his life, he could envisage a future for them all. Now the meeting was over he was able to give her what he knew she wanted—a commitment which the initial ceremony hadn't conveyed.

He thrust his hands in his pockets and walked through the colonnaded walkways of the palace back to the private quarters. He noticed a couple of people look at him quizzically, and he smiled as he realized he'd been whistling under his breath. He couldn't remember the last time he'd done that. What was the tune? One that Ruby had taught Hani.

He continued on past the gardens where Ruby and Hani had first met, pausing at the sand pit as he imagined Ruby in her dress of sunshine yellow, getting splashed with mud and not caring. Her heart always had been bigger than anything else about her. She didn't have a care for all her beauty and glamor, not compared to her love for Hani, which constantly shone through her eyes. It was an expression which he'd tried not to see, tried not to react to. But when that expression had been turned his way, he hadn't stood a chance. He owed it to her not to promise anything he couldn't deliver, but all the work he'd done behind the scenes with the diplomatic mission had finally paid off, and his way was clear to proceed with her coronation—his commitment to her that they had a future together.

He went directly to Hani's room. But the door was open and Hani wasn't resting. He frowned and then he turned around and saw him. He was kneeling by the small fountain, dabbling his fingers in the water as he tried to sail a toy boat. Amir's throat constricted for a moment, as he was overcome by the memory of how Hani had slept for hours at that time of day only months earlier. Now, it seemed, he was full of life and energy.

He went and knelt beside him, not standing over him, hectoring him as he done in recent years, but playing alongside him. Ruby had taught him that.

"You don't feel tired?" asked Amir.

Hani shook his head as he concentrated on righting the boat which had toppled into the water.

"That's good."

Still no answer from Hani as he fiddled with a paper boat which bobbed on the current the flow of water made.

"We have toy boats you could use instead of that."

"Yes, but it's not the same."

It was Amir's turn to frown. "Same as what?"

"Same as the one Ruby made. The one Rat sailed down the river on."

"What?"

"Rat." Hani sighed and picked up the small boat, testing the soggy bottom against his hand. "In *The Wind in the Willows*."

"The wind in the willows?" Amir didn't have the first clue what Hani was talking about.

"It's an old book. One of Grandmother's. Ruby said it was also a favorite of her mother's who read it to Ruby all the time."

"Oh, I see." He didn't, though.

Hani sat back and looked at Amir, a patient look on his face. "Ruby said that if I ever wanted to feel close to her, then all I had to do was think about Rat and Badger and Mole and all the rest of them, and know that she loved them, too."

Amir stood up and frowned, looking across the hills. High above them a plane rose from the airport and swept away in the bright white sky, disappearing into a speck in an instant. "Well, that's a nice idea," he said vaguely, still unsure what his son was talking about. "But you could also go find her. She won't be far away."

Hani just stared at him, as if it were his father who'd gone mad.

"What is it?" Amir pressed his hand to Hani's forehead, thinking he must be sicker than he'd imagined.

"Don't you know? She's gone."

Dread plunged like a stone in Amir's gut, making him feel hot and cold and nauseous all at the same time. The pause lengthened and he licked his lips. Different possibilities shot through his brain. She'd gone shopping; she'd gone to visit someone; she'd… But there were no other options. She knew hardly anyone in Janub Havilah. But he didn't need words, because it was there in his son's stark expression.

"She's gone," Amir repeated. He nodded, once then twice and then again, as if trying to understand the words he'd just uttered.

"Yes."

"Hani…" The word emerged strained and hoarse. He cleared his throat. "Hani," he said, stronger now. "When did she leave?"

Hani shrugged. "Earlier on. I don't know… when I was resting. She came to say goodbye."

Amir gave up any pretense that he knew what was going on. "Did she say where?"

Hani fingered the paper boat in his hands. He shrugged. "Somewhere where she came from, I think. England?" He squinted up at Amir in question.

Amir just about managed a reassuring smile and squeeze of the shoulders. "That's right. She's from England. She's probably gone to see someone."

"I guess."

"Yes, that's what she'll have done." Amir twisted around and glanced toward his bedroom window and hers, with the shared balcony shadowed by the palm tree which dipped and shuddered in the breeze. He could just picture her there, as he'd found her last night. And she'd be there again. No doubt. Just a visit. To friends.

Hani's paper boat suddenly became waterlogged and

sank. He looked up at Amir with a panicked gaze. "It's gone! And I can't make another one. Only Ruby can."

"Then she'll make you another one when she returns."

Hani rubbed his watery eyes. "She's not coming back."

"Of course she is. Why wouldn't she?"

"Because she has a job."

From disbelief Amir suddenly felt filled with anger. A job? She'd left him without a word and disappeared to England for a job? And left Hani, too? It was beyond belief! *She* was beyond belief!

If she was trying to prove that she was an independent woman, then she had another think coming. He'd go over there and bring her back himself. He began walking in the direction of his room. But what if that were the wrong thing to do? He stopped dead in his tracks and thrust his fingers through his hair as he tried to urge his black and white mind to shift into shades of gray. To think like Ruby. Not like shades of gray then, but the colors of a rainbow. The colors of a rainbow he'd failed to see. He was so focused on what he needed to do that he'd overlooked one of the most important things which was happening right before him.

He'd dismissed her fears because he didn't understand them.

He'd ignored her questions, believing them to be ridiculous.

But she'd been afraid and had wanted answers and he'd refused to help her on either count.

Or... maybe, just maybe, she was rejecting this life he'd laid out for her and was returning to her old life. He ground his teeth. He'd offered her everything and she'd thrown it back in his face.

No, she wasn't that crazy. She'd return. All he had to do was wait.

BUT THE WAITING turned into weeks and there was still no word to him from Ruby. To Hani, yes. But intense speculation over every word she wrote to Hani yielded him no further understanding of what was going on.

He watched her every interview, pored over the magazine features in which she modeled, trying to figure out what she was doing. It was only after five weeks had slipped by that he found a clue, his first, in an interview with a gossip magazine. The journalist had discovered she'd recently been to Janub Havilah and was asking her about whether the women were subjugated by the rulers. She'd defended the country and him. And, after being pushed, she'd stated that it was her favorite place in the world.

He'd pushed aside the computer and immediately summoned his assistant. It might not be a declaration of love, but, after so long without anything, and with his own feelings growing clearer, day by day, he knew that he'd have to take a leap of faith. He may be rejected, he may be reviled, but he'd turn up anyway.

HE'D TOLD Hani that this was something he had to do on his own. And, somehow, Hani had accepted the explanation as if he understood. He had Ruby's mind of many shades and colors, not like his rigid, black and white one. And he was glad that Hani wasn't here now. He walked up the rain-slicked street and paused outside the flashing lights of a nightclub. It seemed she hadn't changed her ways. But then, he didn't want her to anymore.

He opened the door and was immediately allowed through, his way paved as usual by his executive assistant, who'd contacted the club beforehand. He'd let him, because he didn't want anything to get in the way of his plan.

It took a while for his eyes and ears to adjust to the gloom and pumping music. Bodies moved rhythmically under the strobe lights while all around, tiered floors held tables and chairs around which beautiful people gathered, drinking and dining. He looked at where most people were—the dance floor. She'd be there.

He pushed his way through, examining everyone as he went, but he didn't find who he was looking for. He emerged on the far side and glanced around at the tables which over-looked the dance floor. She'd have attracted a group of people, and he looked for a vivid blonde head in their midst. But still he drew a blank.

Maybe he'd been given the wrong information by her agency. He walked to the bar and ordered a drink, asking the waitress if he knew of Ruby. She looked vaguely disap-pointed that he was after a particular woman.

"Sure," she said, topping up his drink. "She'll be out there, as usual."

He followed her gaze to the rear of the bar, where a door opened onto a terrace overlooking a small urban garden. Tall trees and climbers had created an oasis which overlooked a small square of grass below, with a fountain at its center. A few minutes passed before his eyes accustomed themselves to the gloom and he saw her.

She stood in the shadows, hands gripped the railing as she looked across the garden toward the moon, which could just be seen through the bare branches of the trees which lined the garden. He wouldn't have seen her except that her cheek, as she leaned forward, caught the lights of the city, which she was looking away from. That she was looking away from the lights didn't escape his notice. She'd always been drawn to them like a bee to honey, like a lonely person seeking company, like a woman terrified of the depression which had dogged her mother. But now she was still, alone and contemplating the moon.

He stepped forward and she started, but didn't turn around. In fact she stilled even more, if that were possible, as if a thought had struck her. Then she shrugged lightly and returned her gaze to the moon.

"Ruby," he said softly, almost unwilling to disturb her unusual reverie. She half-turned her head as if the same thought had returned. He repeated her name once more and this time she twisted around and faced him. The whites of her eyes shone in the dark, making her look even more startled than she was.

He took another step toward her but was stopped from getting any further by a table which held a wine glass, where she'd obviously been sitting. He noticed there was only one glass. He liked that. But, even if the table weren't there, he didn't think he'd have the guts to approach her. He'd made a mess of everything. He, who prided himself on logic and careful decision-making, had failed when it had come to the woman he wanted to share the rest of his life with, the woman who was the mother of his child.

"Amir?" she said hesitantly, her head ducking slightly in disbelief. "Is that really you?"

He gave her a quick smile, which soon disappeared as her frown remained. Had he made this journey for nothing? "It is. Were you expecting someone else?" He could have kicked himself as the words tumbled out, revealing the insecurity and macho possessiveness he always felt with her, but didn't want to show, not now, not at this moment. He couldn't risk jeopardizing his mission, too much depended on it.

Her shoulders sagged and she plucked her champagne flute from the table without taking a drink. "And what if I am? You made it plain that your future didn't include me in it."

"No, you're wrong. That is not what I said."

She tilted her head back and gave a jagged sigh, as if it cost her to breathe. She nodded her head. "Okay, tell me what you think you said."

He opened his mouth to speak but suddenly realized he'd created a hole he couldn't extricate himself from. "Maybe it wasn't exactly what I said, as what I omitted to say."

"Ha! Trying to get out of it with semantics now, are we?"

He shook his head. "Ruby. I've traveled over three thousand miles to see you—"

"And you think I should leap into your arms, is that it?"

"No, what I think you should do is to let me speak."

She folded her arms and put her weight on one hip. "Go on then, I'm waiting."

"It may be," he said slicing the air with his hand as if that would make things more definite, "that I didn't consider your feelings—"

"Feelings? So you've come here to indulge my feelings?" She shook her head, anger showing in every jerky movement. "Honey, it's not my feelings I'm concerned with, believe it or not. It's yours; it's Hani's."

She's blind-sided him and he hadn't seen it coming. "This isn't about you," he suggested hesitantly.

"Of course it's about me. But it's more about you and Hani."

"Right..." He licked his lips as he searched her face for signs of a clue as to what she was talking about.

She clicked her tongue and placed her drink on the table. "Do I have to spell it out?"

"I think you do."

"Jesus! Why are men so obdurate?"

"I don't know. It must be in our genes."

"The reason, Amir, why I left is that Hani didn't want a mother, just a friend, and you didn't want a wife, just a lover."

"And you?" he ventured.

"I want to be a wife and mother. I want commitment, Amir, and while we were married technically, you showed no indication of wanting it to last." She huffed out a pent-up sigh. "I've spent my life on edge, scared of my own shadow, searching for a son I'd given away. I hated myself, Amir. But I don't anymore. And that's something you and Hani have given me, whether you knew it or not. I came to London, not only to take on work, but to get help. And I've spent the past few weeks seeing a counselor who has shown me that I'm stronger than I imagine. I'm not scared of life anymore. In fact, I want life. I know what I want and I'm strong enough to walk away if I can't have it." She paused. "Is that plain enough for you?"

He nodded. "I'm sorry, Ruby. So sorry." He hesitated as he wondered which, of the many things he was sorry for, he should elaborate on. She mistook his silence.

"It's okay. There's no need to be sorry for something you can't help." She looked around as if for escape. "Now, if you've quite finished, why don't you go. Although I have to say that three thousand miles is a long way to come simply to apologize."

He reached out for her as she tried to move past him. "Ruby! You know I'm not the best for words." He decided not to comment on her savage grunt of agreement. "But I haven't come here to apologize." He shrugged. "Well, I have, but not only. I wanted to tell you that you were wrong."

She rolled her eyes. "Fine. I'm sure you think I'm wrong about pretty much everything. You've made that much clear. From my decisions, to the company I keep, to my personality—"

"No. Listen to me, will you? There's nothing wrong with

any of them. You're wrong about me." He gripped her hand more tightly. "When I said it wasn't necessary to remain together for Hani's health, I didn't mean that I didn't wish to continue our marriage.

Her expression plainly showed her disbelief. "So you've come here today to tell me you want to remain married after all." She shook her head. "What? Did you ministers decide it would be best for your country after all to continue to be married to a nobody?" She huffed a laugh. "Or maybe they think it's a good idea to be married to a nobody who has the ear of the Press. That's it, isn't it? Your advisors suggest a bit of celebrity will be good for your image."

"You're talking nonsense."

She pulled her hand away. "You always say that when I don't agree with you." She turned and walked, and he suddenly realized he was going to lose her.

"Ruby! Look! Here, I have something for you." She stopped and turned around, but her expression still wasn't trusting. He fumbled in his pocket and brought out the ring case. "It's a ring."

"I can see that."

"But it's no ordinary ring. It's an eternity ring which belonged to my grandmother."

"And, presumably, belonged to Mia until she died." She looked up with a curious expression.

"No. My grandmother made me swear that I would only ever give the ring to the woman I loved, and who I wanted to share my life with." He smiled at the memory. "My grandmother was big on love."

"And *The Wind in the Willows*, too."

"What?"

She grinned then, that beautiful big grin which transfixed photographers, stopped magazine readers mid page, and floored him totally. "Your grandmother sounds an awesome woman."

"She was. You've have liked each other. More than liked, you'd have—"

In one quick movement she stepped forward and placed a finger against his lips. "I think," she said in a low, provocative tone, "that I'm going to put you out of your misery and say the words which you're evidently unused to saying." She rolled onto tiptoes and kissed him and he lost any thread of thought he had. "Amir, will you remain married to me?"

He grunted a laugh. "I thought you'd never ask."

She leaned against him with a sigh. "Take me home."

Five minutes after she should have arrived.

She was late. Amir checked his watch and rolled back onto his heels, fixing his eyes on the intricately tiled wall of the grand reception room of the Royal Palace. The imam didn't meet his eye, no doubt disconcerted by both the international attention the coronation was receiving, and her lateness for the ceremony. So Amir focused on the intricately decorated walls. First one scroll, then another, determined to ground and control the wayward thoughts which rushed through his head. Would she come? He never felt insecure about anything until he'd allowed himself to realize he loved Ruby—heart, body and soul. She was his. And he was afraid she wouldn't turn up.

There were low murmurs and coughs from the people behind him. He wondered whether they were thinking the same as him. Had she had a change of heart?

· · ·

EIGHT MINUTES after she should have arrived.

AMIR SHIFTED his stance and was immediately angry with himself. He had no wish to betray his insecurities to the world. He drew himself up to his full height and inhaled in a long steadying breath.

She'd come. It would be the fault of all the people who'd descended on the palace from around the world. Make-up artists, hairdressers, celebrity bloggers, stylists, photographers, all determined to ensure she looked her best for the world on her big day.

"She'll be here," said Zavian, in a lowered voice. Zavian was always so certain of everything. Despite himself, he was reassured.

"Of course she will," said Roshan who stood on Amir's other side. "She has eyes only for you."

"And you'd know," scoffed Zavian. "No doubt you couldn't believe she wasn't charmed by your own beautiful visage."

Amir shot Roshan a sharp glance. "Have you been flirting with my wife?" he said in a sharp undertone.

Roshan grinned. "I wish. Unfortunately, as I say, I haven't had the opportunity. Nor the inclination," he added, "knowing she was always destined for you."

Amir looked straight ahead once more and grunted. "I'm glad someone knew."

"Well," Roshan said, straightening his army uniform. "You'd have known too, if you'd allowed yourself to see past your pride."

Zavian placed a firm hand on Amir's arm before he could respond. Amir shook his head. "I'm fine. I won't let Roshan anger me this time, not here, not now" said Amir.

Zavian grunted and glanced at his watch. "Not even if your wife-to-be is ten minutes late for her own coronation?"

Ten minutes *after she should have arrived.*

Zavian was right, damn him. He was angry. She wasn't coming. He threw his hands open in a dramatic gesture of surrender and turned around, only to see a small crowd of photographers and other people slowly making their way to him, through the front doors and the circular domed great hall, its opulent tiled walls glittering in the light from the glassed dome roof high overhead. The great hall—with its colors of terracotta, white, and pockets of bright turquoise—should have put his queen in the shade but, as she emerged from her entourage, she outshone everything and everyone.

The sense of excitement and murmurs preceded her, coming toward him like a wave which buoyed his spirits and made him forget his doubts. Hani walked ahead of her, his manner dignified, as if he were aware of the importance of the occasion and determined to not let anyone down. He'd make a fine king one day, thought Amir. Ruby had originally been nervous about telling him that she would be crowned queen in an official ceremony. But Amir knew his son better. Yes, he'd loved and would always love Mia, the woman who'd raised him as her own, but his love was unlimited and it seemed he could easily accommodate 'fun' into his image of a mother. Hani had been as thrilled as Ruby had been nervous.

But there was no sign of nerves in Ruby now. She moved with the confidence of a model and a woman well loved. She wore an exquisite gown, designed with his country's history in mind, and a headdress from which a matching train dragged behind her. Her whole ensemble was the perfect blend of his country's past and present. But her figure was all her own, as was the wide smile and bright eyes.

As she took her place beside him and the excitement finally ebbed away, she leaned in to him. "Sorry I'm late."

He closed his eyes briefly and shook his head. But he couldn't help smiling. And he suddenly realized his whole life would be like this. Him being charmed by her. And he couldn't wait.

EPILOGUE

*E*ver since Ruby had discovered she was pregnant, she'd waited for that shard of fear to slice into her and debilitate her. Every day. Whether she was hanging out with Hani, helping him with his studies—although Amir disputed the word 'help'—or officiating at state banquets, visiting charities or, her favorite, alone in bed with Amir, Ruby felt a frisson of fear, waiting for the axe to fall and shatter her precious new life.

But it didn't.

The weeks passed into months until she found herself here, wandering around the room Amir had insisted on preparing for her at the palace. The grand chamber had been turned into the kind of place where every thought had been given to comfort—both physical and mental. The room had been selected for the light, diffused and soft as it faced the north. There would be no need to draw the curtains against any harsh sunshine. Only a filmy gauzy silk, which fluttered in the breeze of that spring morning, separated the room from the green of the outside gardens. The trees were large

there, and protected the window with a green, fresh shade—
the color of life and hope.

Ruby brushed her fingers along the velvet throw of the
chaise longue, something definitely only for looking at, not
for giving birth to a baby on. She stopped by an adjoining
door, and momentarily gripped the handle. No, all the equipment and stand-by specialists would be in there, if needed,
out of sight so as to not freak her out, not to assist in
plunging her into the depths of depression about which she'd
been so scared. Had been, but no longer. It was still there, but
only like a shadow nudging at the edge of her mind.

She released her hand from the door, and turned to face
the beautiful room once more. The equipment was there if
she needed it, but she hoped this time to do things naturally.
She looked around. She was in a different world, in every
way you could measure it, compared to when she had given
birth to Hani.

She looked over to the bed where Hani lay curled up
reading. He'd just come in from riding—something he'd
had to forgo in recent years due to lack of strength—and
had settled near her. She liked that. Even if they weren't
doing anything, he'd find her and settle nearby with a book.
Their relationship was growing, changing, deepening. Sure
they still had fun, but now, when the fun was over, they
were together as mother and son. Something she cherished
and nurtured with every passing day, especially now that
he'd have a sibling. She didn't want their relationship to
suffer.

"You're looking thoughtful," said Amir, entering the room
behind her.

She turned with a smile. "Is that so strange?"

"Frankly, yes," he said, with an answering smile. Then the
smile turned to a frown. "Is it the baby?"

"What? You think because I look thoughtful I must be

about to give birth?" She raised a playful eyebrow, glancing over to Hani, who looked up from his book with a grin.

"What do you think, Hani?" asked Amir, walking up to him, and looking at the book he was reading. "Do you reckon your mom looks different somehow?"

Ruby was rewarded with a deep look of scrutiny which made Hani look much older than his years. An old soul, she thought, and her heart melted just a little bit more.

Then he nodded. "You're right, Baba. Ruby looks different. Kind of settled."

She raised her eyebrows in surprise. Amir's concern she could put down to his fears over her past history. But Hani? He'd just described exactly how she felt. She *did* feel different, she *did* feel settled.

She gave a laugh which sounded unsure even to her ears. "You two!" But even as she replied she felt the heaviness in her back increase and she sat on the chaise, as if to test it out. She brushed her hand over the luxurious velvet and the gold ormolu trimmings and took a slow breath to ease the pain. When it had eased she fixed a smile and looked back at her two men. Hani had jumped up, looking concerned, and Amir walked briskly over to her, looked at her and turned back to Hani.

"Hani! Go call the doctors. Tell them they're needed."

Before she could remonstrate another blast of pain shot through her body. She looked across at the door behind which lay a phalanx of pain relief, and suddenly she felt that a natural birth wasn't so important after all.

She looked back into Amir's eyes, full of love and concern and a strength she knew she'd need.

"There's nothing to worry about, Ruby. I'm here, Hani's here, and there's nothing to fear. You must trust me."

Then he picked her up and carried her across to the bed, and laid her down as carefully as if she were his most treasured thing in the world. And in that moment, she knew she did trust him. And she knew that all would be well.

AIYSA WAS BORN PREMATURELY but strong and healthy for all that. Ruby pushed herself up to sitting and looked across at Amir, who stood before the window with Aiysa in his arms, smitten from the moment she'd emerged into the world.

There was something enchanting, she thought, about watching a strong and powerful man brought to his knees by a scrap of a baby daughter with healthy lungs.

"Baba looks goofy," said Hani quietly, so his father couldn't hear. He sat on the floor beside her bed where he'd pieced together an elaborate train set.

Ruby laughed. "Goofy? I bet your father's never been called that before. Hm, I think 'besotted' might be a better word."

"What does 'besotted' mean."

"It means full of love."

Hani smiled and gazed at his father once more. "Ah, yes, I see what you mean."

She tousled his hair. "And you know when else he looks besotted?"

He looked up at her with her own eyes. "When?"

"When he looks at you."

Amir looked up at her then.

"And when he looks at you, too," said Hani.

And Ruby knew he was right.

AFTERWORD

Thank you for reading *The Sheikh's Secret Baby*. I hope you enjoyed it! Reviews are always welcome—they help me, and they help prospective readers to decide if they'd enjoy the book.

The other books in the series are:

Bought by the Sheikh
The Sheikh's Forbidden Lover

My other sheikh series is Desert Kings.

Wanted: A Wife for the Sheikh
The Sheikh's Bargain Bride
The Sheikh's Lost Lover
Awakened by the Sheikh
Claimed by the Sheikh
Wanted: A Baby by the Sheikh

If you've read all of the above, why not try out one of my

other books? There is the **Italian Romance** series which begins with *Perfect*. Then there are two series set in New Zealand—**The Mackenzies**, and **New Zealand Brides**. Against a backdrop of beautiful New Zealand locations—deserted beaches, Wellington towers, snow-capped mountains—the Mackenzie and Connelly families fall in love. But expect some twists and turns!

You can check out all my books on the following pages. And, if you'd like to know when my next book is available, you can sign up for my new release e-mail list via my website—https://www.dianafraser.com.

Happy reading!

Diana

~

BOUGHT BY THE SHEIKH

BOOK 2 OF SHEIKHS OF HAVILAH—
ZAVIAN AND GABRIELLE

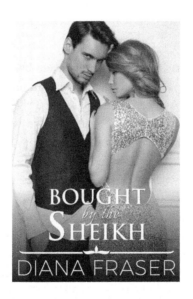

A dysfunctional upbringing has made Sheikh Zavian bin Ameen Al Rasheed distrustful of people—but he trusted Gabrielle. That is, until she betrayed him by accepting his father's bribe to leave Zavian and his country. He's left shattered by the betrayal but with an obsession for her which only increases with time.

Raised by her eccentric grandfather in the deserts of Taraq, Gabrielle loves the country and Zavian so much that she leaves them. He's to become King and he needs to marry a suitable Bedouin. So she accepts Zavian's father's bribe to leave—it was the only way to make sure Zavian didn't follow her—and, in so doing, exiles herself from the only home and man she's ever loved.

But a year later, as wedding plans are underway, Zavian suspects Gabrielle is the 'anonymous' donor of one his country's most precious artifacts, purchased for the exact sum as the bribe. So he buys her services from her university in order to find out the truth and rid himself of his obsession. Besides, if Gabrielle can't be his wife, then why not his mistress?

Excerpt

She felt a prickle down her neck and back which settled low inside her. The silk of her abaya shimmered slightly as the air shifted. A door clicked closed and she swung around. He was formally dressed in a white gown which made him appear even taller than he was. She'd always loved the traditional robes. They had a simplicity and a beauty which was timeless. Every eye in the room had moved to Zavian when he wore European clothes, but the clothes of a king? He was not only magnetic, but awesome. This wasn't a man to cross. This wasn't her man any longer, not the man with whom she'd discovered the objects.

The prickle that had begun in her neck sunk lower into her gut as Zavian walked towards her.

"Zavian!" His name rushed from her lips before she could check it. She could feel the color rushing to her cheeks as he continued to gaze on her with a hunger which made her feel weak. She couldn't allow herself to be sucked in by it, to forget why they could never be together. Somehow she found the control and stepped away, needing space between them. "Your Majesty."

As she uttered the honorific, the look in his eyes changed, and the arrogant control that she'd witnessed the previous evening returned.

"Ms Taylor."

His formality cut to the heart of her, but she refused to allow him to see it. As far as he was concerned she'd been bribed to leave him and his country, and she'd disappeared from his life without a farewell.

"I see you've been admiring some of my private collection."

She gasped lightly as he lifted his hand and reached past her. She froze, all her senses acutely attuned to him, wondering what he was going to do. But he simply retrieved one of the objects she'd been looking at and held it up to the light, twisting it in his strong hands, hands whose sensitivity she remembered well.

"I admire this piece for its simplicity."

Taking advantage of his switch in focus, she exhaled lightly and composed herself. "I... I've never considered it to be simple."

The corners of his lips tweaked slightly but he didn't shift his gaze from the piece. "It's contours are regular, its shape standard to its type. How could it *not* be considered simple?" he asked, passing it to her, their fingers touching.

"Because..." She paused willing herself to focus on the piece, not him. "Because every time I look at it I see something different." She twisted the piece in the light. "A shade, a line, a ridge, a measurement of time etched into its fabric. Something beautiful, and yet flawed, all together in one piece."

She looked from the piece to him. He'd lowered his eyes which were now focused on her lips. When he raised them again, their chestnut hue was darker than before. "You always did make something simple, complex."

"Perhaps because it was never simple."

A muscle flickered in his jaw but he said nothing. "You're wrong, you know. Everything is simple; everything can be reduced down to essentials."

"Why is that so important to you?"

"Because only then can you judge it, can you assess it for what it really is."

She shook her head. He was too near for her to think clearly. His eyes roamed her face as the silence lengthened, deepened and became unbearable. She swallowed and stood a little straighter.

"Well, I wish you luck with that. What is it you wanted to see me about, Your Majesty?" She hoped by using his title she'd remind them both that the easy intimacy of their conversation needed to stop.

He walked up to her and it took all of her willpower not to retreat. He stopped in front of her. Too close. "I paid a lot of money to bring you here and yet you demand to know why I wish to meet you?" His eyes hooded and he cocked his head a little to one side. "I thought you knew all about the power of money."

She wished she didn't blush so easily, but the guilt and tragedy around his comment sent floods of blood pulsing through her, branding her with guilt. But there was nothing she could do to defend herself. She needed to be guilty in his eyes. "Indeed."

"And the person with the money has the control, isn't that so?"

She nodded. His proximity was making it hard for her to think straight. "Sometimes," she muttered.

"I think you'll find it's true all the time. Otherwise why would you be here?"

"But why me? There were others who could have done this job. Others without the complications I bring."

"Sometimes, unfortunately, complications cannot be avoided, they have to be faced in order to make things simple once more. There are things, Gabrielle, I need to know. Beginning with this." He picked up a remote control and pressed a button. A part of the wall slid away revealing the Sana'a Quran.

Stunned, she stepped back as if pushed by a force field. She'd assumed it had been locked away somewhere in the most secure part of the museum. She'd assumed wrong. She was faced with her weakness—a way to absolve herself from accepting the bribe, a way to return a treasure to its rightful place, a way she'd thought had been anonymous.

Maybe it was a fake? She walked up to it, heartbeat quickening, but could see at a glance it was genuine. The telltale marks of ancient Arabic and the particular shades of color used by the Bedouin thousands of years ago proved it was the original, which meant someone had linked her to it.

When she looked back at him, his eyes had changed. He knew. He absolutely knew. He might be inscrutable, but she was an open book to him. He motioned her to sit at the table, in front of the Sana'a Quran. She had no option but to do so, to sit and look at the object which had betrayed her.

He stood beside her. "It's beautiful, isn't it?"

"Yes," she said from between tight lips.

"And mysterious."

She twisted her lips close as if scared the truth would come tumbling out.

"Don't you agree?"

She shrugged. "Not really. We know where it came from."

"Yes, but we don't know how it came here, do we?"

She shrugged. "I don't see how I can help you there." She kept her eyes firmly on him, refusing to give him the satisfaction of looking away, but all the while knowing that her bright red cheeks betrayed her.

"Do you not?"

She shrugged. "The provenance is well known."

"Not to me."

"It was found not far from here, I believe."

"Among the ruins of Sana'a. Yes, thank you. *That* much I do know."

"And then it went missing."

"I'm so pleased that I spent so much money to bring you here, to get such an incisive background to the piece. Although I'm not sure your Oxford College will be as pleased."

The reminder that her Oxford department depended on her work, and that its future and hers depended on the King was timely. She swallowed. "What else do you want to know?"

"I've told you. About the book. I want you to tell me what happened to it. How it came to be part of my collection." He sighed and sat down, frowning, his hands steepled before him.

She opened her mouth to speak but the words eluded her.

"Tell me," he repeated.

"I can't."

"I thought you might say that. You have one month, Gabrielle. One month in which to provide the stories my PR department requires. There are four pieces, including this one. And I want the truth about them before you leave."

"And if I can't discover the truth."

"Then your Oxford College will not receive payment for your services and will cease to exist."

"How do you know—"

"That your College is desperately short of funds? It came

to my attention that one of its major sources of funds had dried up."

She closed her eyes briefly. "It was you."

He shrugged. "I do what I have to do." He stepped away. "You have a month, Gabrielle. One month until the millennia celebrations when your paid services will no longer be required."

"Why then?"

"Because I will then know exactly what I need to know."

As he swept out the room, she knew with absolute certainty that he wouldn't allow her to leave Gharb Havilah without giving him what he wanted. But, if she did that, she risked damaging the very country she loved.

~

Buy Now!

ALSO BY DIANA FRASER

Desert Kings

Wanted: A Wife for the Sheikh

The Sheikh's Bargain Bride

The Sheikh's Lost Lover

Awakened by the Sheikh

Claimed by the Sheikh

Wanted: A Baby by the Sheikh

The Sheikhs of Havilah

The Sheikh's Secret Baby

Bought by the Sheikh

The Sheikh's Forbidden Lover

The Mackenzies

The Real Thing

The PA's Revenge

The Marriage Trap

The Cowboy's Craving

The Playboy's Redemption

The Lakehouse Café

New Zealand Brides

Yours to Give

Yours to Treasure

Yours to Cherish

Italian Romance

Perfect

Her Retreat

Trusting Him

An Accidental Christmas

Made in the USA
Las Vegas, NV
10 March 2021